The Princess School

Apple-y Ever After

Jane B. Mason · Sarah Hines Stephens

SCHOLASTIC INC.

New York Toronto London Auckland Sydney
Mexico City New Delhi Hong Kong Buenos Aires

For our five sisters, neither step nor evil,
for keeping us on our toes.

— JBM & SHS

Published by Scholastic Inc.

ISBN 0-439-69814-6

12 11 10 9 8 7 6 5 4 3 2 6 7 8 9 10/0

Printed in the U.S.A. 40

First printing, September 2005

Chapter One
Bluebird

"Mmm . . . hmmmm." Snow White's cheery hum turned into a long sigh as she sat down on the cushion of her chair. The simple song she had been thinking of was not making her smile as it usually did.

Smiling felt like a great effort, yet Snow's lips arced up automatically toward her pink cheeks when she saw her friends Briar Rose, Cinderella Brown, and Rapunzel Arugula come through the classroom door. They all smiled too and waved at her, but the moment they took their seats, Snow's mouth drooped and she sighed again, more loudly. Feeling blue took a lot out of her.

Ducking behind the piled-up hairdo of the princess in front of her, Snow propped her heavy head on her hands while Madame Garabaldi, the first-year Bloomers' hearthroom teacher, rapped out scroll call. It just wasn't like Snow to feel down, especially here at

Princess School. She loved learning how to be a proper princess, especially with Ella, Rapunzel, and Rose in her class. Normally, Snow woke up smiling and excited to skip off to school. But this morning she had woken up uneasy. She wasn't sure what could be the matter or how to make herself feel glad again.

Snow gazed through the tall, diamond-paned window, hoping to spot a happy distraction. Normally a simple glimpse of a flitting bird or a squirrel on a branch would make Snow giggle and clap her hands with delight. But not this morning.

With her chin in her palm, Snow counted at least three bluebirds winging outside without cracking a smile. Even as the birds came closer and closer, swooping and flapping, Snow remained glum.

She watched the birds land on the window ledge and bob their tiny heads as if they were watching her through the glass.

"Snow White!" Madame Garabaldi called loudly.

"Yes?" Snow White sat up straight. She had been so busy watching the birds she forgot about scroll call. "I mean, present . . . Madame," she added.

"I'm quite pleased to hear it," Madame Garabaldi said evenly. "For a moment I felt certain you were somewhere else." Her steely gaze rested on the top of Snow's carved wooden desk. "Elbows off," she said crisply.

Snow blushed and put her hands in her lap. She

had to be especially careful around Madame Garabaldi so as not to let the hearthroom teacher see the bad habits Snow had picked up from the dwarves. Mort, Meek, Hap, Nod, Wheezer, Dim, and Gruff were loads of fun and loved Snow dearly, but they were not very regal-mannered.

As soon as the instructor lowered her eyes to the scroll-call parchment, Snow turned back to the window. The bluebirds were still there, looking in more intently than ever. One of them tapped lightly on the glass, and a moment later the other two joined in.

They sound as if they're knocking to be admitted! Snow thought, managing a small grin. She could not shake the feeling that they were looking at her. And she wasn't the only one who noticed.

Ella turned and leaned across the aisle.

"Snow, I think those birds are trying to tell you something!" she said in a hushed whisper.

"Oh, I'm sure they aren't here for me," Snow whispered back. She had befriended each and every bird throughout the land, but what would they want with her while she was in class?

THUNK!

All of the girls in the chamber jumped as a large tern landed heavily on the sill, spotted Snow White, and joined in tapping on the glass.

Snow's brow furrowed uncharacteristically. She had

to admit that the birds were most certainly focused on her. So was Madame Garabaldi, and she clearly was not amused by the rapping and flapping fowl. Snow felt her pale face redden again as the stern teacher looked from her to the growing aviary outside.

Flustered, Snow motioned the birds away with her hand. But they kept pecking, louder and louder. When the instructor's back was turned, Snow quickly stood and made flapping gestures with her pale arms.

"Fly away," she whispered desperately. "Fly away!"

A few of the other Bloomers in class giggled, but Snow's friends looked befuddled and concerned. And the birds . . . well, either they could not understand or they did not want to.

At the front of the chamber, Madame Garabaldi read a long list of announcements from an ivory scroll. Snow wasn't able to concentrate on a single one. *Tap . . . tap . . . tappity . . . tap-tappity.* The pecking continued like a strange percussion performance. More and more birds arrived. Soon seagulls were circling and screeching loudly with their laughterlike call. Robins, budgies, and other small birds chimed in with more delicate tweets. Crows cawed and owls screeched. And all of them took turns pecking at the window. It was like a symphony gone awry.

"Snow, can't you do something?" Rose whispered from the next aisle.

Several Bloomers were staring open-mouthed at the mass of birds on the windowsill. And none of them was even pretending to listen to their teacher.

"Maybe we should let them in," Rapunzel said with a mischievous grin.

Finally Madame Garabaldi grabbed the golden tassel holding back the velvet drapes. With a flick of her wrist, she let the tassel fall free, and the heavy curtains swung over the glass. Snow caught a glimpse of several huge pelicans gliding in for a landing before the birds disappeared behind the velvet.

The light in the room grew dim and the noise of the birds became a bit muffled. "Grimm nonsense." Madame Garabaldi frowned.

"Yes, Grimm," Snow repeated softly. It was certainly possible that the witches who attended the nearby Grimm School were stirring up potions that would make the birds act strangely. Still, Snow was not convinced. It really seemed that the birds were trying to communicate something to her . . . something important.

Madame Garabaldi clapped her hands rapidly and a page stepped forward from the back of the room. He looked a bit guilty as he tried to hide a yawn and straighten his pointy hat.

"This is an awful nuisance!" Madame Garabaldi stated as she wrote something on a small scroll. "Lady

Bathilde must be informed of this disturbance at once."

Taking the scroll, the page bowed several times and backed out of the chamber. Snow did not envy his task of bringing bad news to the headmistress.

When the trumpet sounded to mark the end of class, the princesses filed delicately into the marble halls, whispering behind gloved hands about the birds' strange behavior. Snow found herself surrounded by her own flock of non-feathered friends. They padded together over the polished pink-and-white tile floor.

"What do you know, Snow?" Rapunzel asked in her usual frank manner.

"Nothing," Snow said, biting her lower lip to keep from crying. She was feeling terribly nervous.

"Can you think of any reason those birds would be here to see you?" Rose asked gently.

Ella, Rapunzel, and Rose all looked at Snow expectantly. She could tell they had noticed she felt shaken.

Snow opened her mouth to answer Rose, but before anything came out there was a clatter of claws and beaks on the window beside them.

"Goodness!" Snow exclaimed, alarmed. She turned toward the birds. "Shoo!" Snow said sweetly to the seagulls clamoring at the glass. "*Please* shoo!" she begged. Out of the corner of her eye, Snow saw Lady

Bathilde hurrying down the corridor with an unusual scowl on her face.

"I'll have to have the groundskeeper purchase extra cleaning supplies," Snow heard the elegant headmistress declare. "The excess excrement must not permanently stain the castle!"

Snow heard Rapunzel's stifled laugh and turned back toward the window. The gulls were gazing through the glass at her with such imploring looks that it was undeniably clear. The birds were here for her. But what did they want, and how could she prevent them (and herself) from getting into trouble?

Chapter Two
Flurry of Feathers

The day dragged on. By lunchtime there were so many birds swarming the school that the princesses could not be allowed into the courtyard. The curtains were closed in every classroom chamber, but that did little to shut out the noise of the feathered creatures. Screeches, squawks, and caws filled nearly every castle chamber.

Snow could not focus at all — even during the last class of the day, when Madame Istoria announced a special assignment. It was simply too difficult to pay attention.

"For the rest of the week, your Princesses Past and Present classes will be combined with Stitchery class." The petite, dark-haired instructor beamed. "Each of you will research your ancestors and create a family tree. Once you have completed the historical portion on parchment, you will stitch your trees onto cloth, creating a royal heirloom!"

Snow felt dazed as the instructor clapped her hands together excitedly. All around her, other novice princesses began whispering about the assignment.

Madame Istoria held her hand up, palm out, and the girls quickly quieted down. "If all goes well, these family tree projects will be displayed at our Royal Family Open Castle in the spring."

The chamber once again came alive with excited whispers, and Snow pondered the family tree assignment. Should she focus on her father's family, or the dwarves? She certainly didn't want to learn anything more about her awful stepmother, Queen Malodora.

Suddenly Snow was jolted by a horrible thought. What if Malodora was up to something dreadful? Were the birds trying to warn her that she was in danger? Or worse, were they themselves in danger? Oh, the poor winged creatures!

Forcing her hands back into her lap, Snow tried to banish her last thought. Malodora had barely crossed her mind lately. In fact Snow had not felt that creepy, icy feeling that Malodora was watching her since the Maiden Games, when Snow had stood up to the awful queen. But now just thinking of Malodora sent chills running down her spine like drips from the tip of an icicle.

Ever since the games Snow had pushed all her fears and bad memories away, warming herself in the love and affection of her adopted dwarf family and Ella, Rapunzel, and Rose. Although she'd successfully stood up to the queen once with her friends' support, there was a lot she had not yet dealt with — a lot she did not want to deal with.

Snow could not bring herself to face what her stepmother had done to her father. Malodora, a powerful sorceress and the headmistress of the Grimm School, had most certainly cast some sort of wicked spell on him with her enchanted mirror, for her father had been away at sea for a long, long time. Sometimes Snow dreamed of him at the helm of a ship in a storm, calling her name as the ship moved farther and farther away.

It was too horrible. Snow could not bring herself to think about the evil deeds Malodora had done or was capable of doing. She could not bear how much she missed her father. Nor could she take not knowing what was going on with the birds outside. It was all too much.

At last the final trumpet sounded. Holding back a sob, Snow raced out of the classroom, down the corridor, and out the castle doors onto the drawbridge. Her friends were right on her heels.

Birds flew down from every branch, windowsill, and turret to land on or near Snow. They nearly covered her, tugging at her hair and clothes and squawking loudly in her ears.

From inside the flurry of feathers Snow heard her friends' voices.

"What should we do?" Rose cried.

"What do they want?" Ella asked.

"Maybe I should get a net," Rapunzel suggested.

Snow allowed the birds to tug her along. They were urging her off the bridge and down the lane, away from the school castle. Ducking under a flapping wing, Snow called to the other girls as she ran.

"They want me to go with them!" she yelled over the squawks. She rushed along the lane with the birds flying beside and above her. Snow was moving so quickly, she almost felt like she was flying.

"There's nothing down this way but the harbor," Snow called back to her friends, who were growing smaller in the distance.

"Wait! We'll come, too!" Snow heard Ella call back. Snow slowed, but the bluebird on her shoulder whistled so beseechingly that she picked up her pace again.

"I can't wait!" Snow yelled. "I don't know what it is, but it must be terribly important!"

Chapter Three
Friend or Fowl?

Rose looked from Ella's worried eyes to the small figure of Snow White surrounded by a flock of birds shrinking in the distance. She didn't need to look at Rapunzel. Nor did she need to speak. Rose, Rapunzel, and Ella took off after their friend. Whether the birds were being helpful or not, something strange was happening and they could not let Snow face it alone.

Rapunzel pulled ahead of the other girls and nimbly vaulted the low wall surrounding the school grounds. Ella climbed it gracefully and jumped to the other side. Following close behind, Rose gathered her skirts in one hand and prepared to leap. But at the last moment something snagged her slipper. Her leg tangled in a trailing rose branch and she fell ungracefully to the ground.

"Blasted brambles!" Rose exclaimed so loudly that several of the princesses still on the school bridge turned to look at her and covered their mouths with their hands. They were not accustomed to hearing "Beauty" raise her voice, let alone use unprincesslike language.

She knew her outburst was unregal, but Rose truly hated being pricked by thorns. And she didn't much care for falling, either. She was glad her fussing guardian fairies weren't around to see it.

Well, I can't help Snow if I'm flat on the ground, Rose thought, picking herself up. *Though by now the others are probably so far ahead I'll have lost them.*

Pulling the prickly plant away from her silken shoes, Rose was surprised to see a lightly freckled hand reaching to help.

"I almost tripped on that, too." Rapunzel's eyes were smiling as she stooped to untangle Rose. "It seems like the whole school is getting a bit overgrown," she added.

Rose knew Rapunzel was just trying to make her feel better, but what she'd said was true. Rose had noticed the plants on the castle grounds seemed to be growing out of control lately. The normally immaculately manicured lawns had clumps of dandelions. Weeds were spreading between the stones in the garden paths, and ivy was creeping up the castle walls. Rose smiled and let Rapunzel pull her to her feet. "Thanks," she said.

In the distance she could still see Ella, but Snow

had disappeared over the rise. The only sign of her was the cloud of birds flying high above her head.

Rose regathered her skirts, took a few steps, and jumped. This time she landed gracefully with both feet together on the other side of the wall. She turned to smile at Rapunzel, who was nodding her approval. "Hurry or we'll never catch up," Rose said.

Rapunzel scrunched her mouth to one side. Then she began running the other way. "You go ahead. I have an idea," she shouted over her shoulder.

Rose paused for a moment then sprinted as quickly as she could after Ella and Snow. Rapunzel had some pretty wild schemes sometimes. But Rose had spent enough time with her to know that they usually worked. If Rapunzel had needed Rose's help, she would have asked for it. Besides, at the moment it was Snow who needed her.

Running like the wind, Rose drew closer to Ella. The sound of her footsteps and her heartbeat drummed in her ears. She heard other footsteps, too. Loud, pounding ones. Rose looked hard at Ella's feet just ahead. What kind of shoes was the poor girl wearing? Iron boots? Rose would not put such footwear past Ella's awful stepmother!

But a moment later Rose realized that the clomping sound was not coming from Ella's feet. It was the sound of hoofbeats!

Rapunzel rode up alongside Rose, bareback, on a jet-black mare. She was leading a chestnut horse with a white blaze behind her. "I borrowed them from the Princess School stables," Rapunzel explained, trying to tuck a loose lock of her incredibly long auburn mane behind one ear. Reaching down with her free hand, she helped Rose swing up in front of her before tossing the reins of the other horse to Ella.

"Great idea," Ella said, panting. "Snow is practically flying with those birds. I don't know if we would ever have caught up with her."

"We will now." Rapunzel gave her horse a light prod with her heel and they galloped after Snow.

Rose squinted ahead at the cloud of birds. "It looks like Snow was right," she called out. "They're leading her straight to the harbor." Rose suddenly realized that most of the flock were seabirds — terns, gulls, pelicans, and egrets. And the closer they got to the shore, the louder the birds called.

Rose felt Rapunzel stiffen behind her. "Rose," Rapunzel said in a worried voice, "isn't Snow's father lost at sea?"

Rose nodded, feeling the dread rise in her throat. "But if he has come back, wouldn't the birds sound . . . happier?"

Rapunzel said nothing, but nudged the horse with her heels once more to urge it to run faster.

When they finally reached the harbor, Snow was standing at the shore, gasping for breath. Most of the birds had scattered. Only the seagulls remained, screeching over her head and wheeling out over the open water. Rose noticed with relief that, now that Snow had reached the water, the birds seemed calmer.

"Oh, it would be nice to have wings!" Snow cried breathlessly. Ella helped her onto the chestnut horse and the four friends steered their horses toward the pier.

"Why did the birds lead you here?" Ella asked.

"I'm not sure," Snow said, petting the horse and looking toward the water's edge. "Perhaps it's about my father."

Rose saw Snow gulp. "Do you think he might have come home?" she asked, her hands shaking slightly.

Snow's eyes filled with tears. Her lips disappeared — pressed together tightly. Rose understood. The return of Snow's father, King White, was just too much for her to hope for.

Rapunzel slid off her horse and approached a fisherman mending his nets. "Excuse me," she said. The fisherman looked up, surprised to see so many girls in finery at the harbor. He removed his cap. "Have any boats docked here recently?" Rapunzel asked.

"No, miss. I'm afraid not. The weather has been

terrible," he replied. "I'd have to say that more ships have been sunk than anchored of late."

Rose drew in a sharp breath and looked at Snow's face. But Snow wasn't paying attention. Her head was cocked toward the wharf.

"What is it, Snow?" Ella asked.

"Listen!" Snow said. She seemed almost excited.

All Rose could hear were the screeching gulls and a barking sea lion.

"That sea lion hasn't stopped barking since we arrived!" Snow hopped down from the horse, turning to give it a kiss on the flank and a pat of thanks for the ride. Then she ran as fast as she could in skirts over sand, under the wharf to where the sea lion was waiting.

"Hold on!" Rose slid down to follow her.

"I never knew Snow was so fast!" Rapunzel said as she and Ella tied up the horses then rushed to catch up.

Before they could reach her, Snow was moving toward the waves with the sea lion at her side. Without a word or a look back, she plunged into the frigid water and hugged the animal around the neck.

"Snow!" Ella gasped.

Rose stopped where she was and watched as Snow and the sea lion swam swiftly to the spot in the water below the circling birds.

"What is she doing? Rapunzel exclaimed worriedly. She shook her head. "It's a terrible time of year for a swim," she added. But her eyes were growing wider. "What is that?"

Rose was about to ask the same thing. Snow and the sea lion were nudging something back toward the shore. It looked like a log, or maybe the planking from a ship — and on top of it was a motionless lump.

"Is that a person?" Ella asked breathlessly.

Rapunzel, Rose, and Ella waded out to help. Rose gasped as they got closer. It was a person — a man. Together the four girls pulled the poor wretch out of the water.

Rose's skirts were heavy with icy water, but she barely noticed. She could not take her eyes off the waterlogged man. His long dark hair streaked with gray hung out of his striped sailor's hat. A wet shaggy beard covered most of his face. He did not look like a king. Worse, he did not look alive.

Rose held Ella's hand as they gazed at the soaked sailor. Was he . . . could he possibly be . . . Snow's father? Rose was afraid to even ask the question.

Kneeling beside his limp body, Snow leaned slowly over and kissed the man on the forehead. As Snow's lips touched his face, his eyes fluttered open. Rose gasped.

Snow did not need to say a word. The sailor's warm, dark eyes fringed in black lashes were the image of Snow's own. The raven-haired princess threw her arms tightly around the near-drowned man. "Father!" she cried.

Chapter Four
Father?

Snow hugged her father as tightly as she could and hoped with all her heart that she was not dreaming. She did not want to let him go ever again. Gently, the sopping sire eased Snow off of him and sat up. "Where am I?" he asked.

Snow was a little surprised that her father didn't recognize his own harbor. But he had been away for a long time. And his journey home had clearly been treacherous.

"You've come home!" Snow clapped her hands together joyfully and got to her feet. "At last you've come home." She beamed at her father and grabbed his hand. How wonderful it was to have him near!

"Home?" Confusion shone in the poor man's eyes. He looked pale, Snow noticed, even for a cold, near-drowned member of the White family. His beard and hair were extremely long and he was terribly slim. He was not the clean-cut, broad-shouldered father she remembered, but Snow would have known him anywhere. She hugged him again, completely overcome with happiness.

"Who are you?" he asked plainly.

Snow giggled. In her excitement she had completely forgotten to introduce her friends! "Golly! This is Rapunzel Arugula, Cinderella Brown, and Briar Rose." Snow's dripping friends curtsied in turn. "They are my best friends from school." There was so much to catch up on she was not sure where to begin. He didn't know anything about the dwarves or her cottage or Princess School or . . .

"And you?" her father asked, looking straight at Snow. "Who are you?"

Snow could feel her mouth hanging open. She was too shocked to close it. Surely he was joking. She waited for him to laugh. To hug her. "Why, I am your daughter, Snow White!"

Snow's father just smiled weakly. He reached up and touched Snow's cheek. "I have dreamed of a daughter as fair as you, dear girl. But I have spent my life at sea. I have no daughter."

Speechless, Snow turned her gaze on her friends. They looked as horrified as she did. She was not sure what to say or do next. How could her father not remember her?

"Of course you have a daughter," Rapunzel said,

placing a steady hand on Snow's shoulder as she smiled at King White. "You just need to warm up by the fire."

"Perhaps a bowl of soup and a change of clothes will improve your memory," Ella added. She gently prodded King White over to the chestnut horse and helped him on.

"He's just in shock," Rose said, putting her arm around Snow. "He'll soon remember."

"Let's get him to your cottage." Rapunzel boosted Ella and Rose onto the black mare.

Snow allowed herself to be hoisted up behind her father. She held him around the waist so she would not slip off. She barely felt her cold, sodden clothes as Rapunzel led the mare down the lane toward the dwarves' cottage. Everything felt so strange, like a hazy dream. How could she have her father back and yet not have him at all? He *had* to remember her. Snow hugged him tighter, and tried to believe that it would all be okay soon.

When the horses arrived at the cottage, several of the dwarves were waiting outside.

Gruff eyed the pack of riders warily. "No one told me we'd have guests," he grumbled.

Snow smiled despite her worries. Gruff's familiar grumpiness was a welcome relief.

"Snow, dear! What's this?" Mort said, clapping his

hands together. "What a surprise. Good to see you, my dears!" Mort greeted Ella, Rapunzel, and Rose warmly. "And who's this?" His eyes fell on Snow's father and suddenly registered concern. "Wait, no time for introductions. You are soaked to the bone! Get to the fire quickly, and then you can tell us everything."

The dwarves crowded around the girls and King White and bustled them inside to warm up. Mort brought out a towering stack of blankets and Wheezer put the kettle on for tea. Snow led her father to the fire and wrapped a blanket around his shoulders. He still looked a bit dazed, but he thanked her politely and seemed pleased to be standing near the warmth. Dim peered up at the wet man so intently Snow could tell it was making her father nervous.

"Hap, please wake up Nod," she said. "Meek, it's okay, you can come out from behind that chair. I have someone important I want you to meet. This is my father, King Alabaster White."

The dwarves glanced at one another, wide-eyed and silent, before coming closer and staring at the man who stood dripping in their living room.

"Father, these are my . . . dwarves," Snow said slowly. She wasn't sure she should call them her fathers in front of her true father, even if he didn't know who he was.

King White looked as stunned as the dwarves. He shook his head as if to protest, but said nothing.

"Welcome to our house," Mort said quietly. "Please sit."

King White tried to sit in the small chair Wheezer was holding for him, but at the last moment the snuffly dwarf sneezed and jerked the chair, leaving the king sprawled on the floor.

"Hmph," Gruff said. "Come back from sea, have you? Well, Snow was getting along just fine without you."

Ella turned toward the kitchen. "Why don't I start the soup?" she said.

Snow was grateful for Ella's interruption. She knew Gruff meant well, but sometimes he could be so unfriendly. Luckily her father hadn't seemed to notice.

"Would you like to see the rest of the cottage?" Hap asked. "We could see about finding you some dry clothes."

"That's very kind." King White still seemed to be in a fog but he got up from the floor and followed Hap and Mort upstairs. Meek hurried after him and tugged at his dripping sleeve, then mumbled something at the floor.

"What's that?" King White turned and yelped as he cracked his head against a beam in the low ceiling.

"He said you should watch your head," Hap explained, obviously too late.

Snow could not take her eyes off her father as he disappeared up the stairs. She wanted to wail. She wasn't sure what was worse — to have a missing father or a father missing his memory!

"Don't worry, Snow," Ella said, as if reading her mind. "He could never truly forget you. It's just going to take a little time for him to remember."

Rose and Rapunzel nodded in agreement as they laid out the bowls and spoons. They had just finished setting the table when seven tiny fairies buzzed in through the window. In a swirling whirl of color and high-pitched voices they swarmed around Rose.

"We expected you home hours ago," the blue fairy, Petunia, fussed in Rose's ear. Rose winced and brushed her away like a fly.

"Your father is in a state!" Viola squeaked. "You'd better get home at once."

Rose quieted the fairies with a calm stare. "At this moment, Snow needs me more than I need to get home for supper," she said. "Please tell Father I am perfectly fine and I will be home before dark. He can send a coach for me if he must."

Snow saw Rapunzel nod approvingly. Rose had become so much more independent since the start of school! Snow felt grateful that her friend was staying by her side.

"Sit closer to the fire, Snow," Rose instructed. "I'll go get you a dry gown."

"I'm afraid I have to go now," Rapunzel said. "I need to get the horses back before they are missed!" Rapunzel hugged Snow tightly, then disappeared out the door.

"You had better go, too, Ella," Snow said, still feeling like she was in a dream — or maybe a nightmare. "The soup smells delicious, but you'll be in a stew yourself if you don't get home."

Ella sighed and wiped her hands on a towel. "I know, but —"

"Go. I'll be fine," Snow insisted, trying to sound brave. She wished all of her friends could stay with her, but she knew they needed to get home. And at least she had Rose and the dwarves.

CRACK! King White banged his head again on his way back down. "They're a little small, but they do feel drier," he said, indicating his ridiculously tiny tunic and breeches.

Snow almost laughed. Her father looked like a jester in the dwarf's clothes. And they'd given him things that needed to be mended! There was a large hole in the seat of his breeches and another by his elbow. She would have to sew him something more suitable, and wash and mend his old clothes, too. But right now she was most interested in mending his memory.

"Sit down here, Father," Snow said as cheerfully as she could. "The soup is almost ready. I just know that after a few bites you're going to remember everything!"

Chapter Five
Thornbury Green

Rapunzel tapped her foot impatiently on the Princess School drawbridge. Where were Ella, Rose, and Snow?

Rapunzel had woken early and hurried to school before her good friend Prince Val had even arrived for their usual walk to school together. Rapunzel was hoping to catch her friends before the first trumpet. She wanted to hear if King White had remembered anything. She was tired and anxious, too, for she had spent the whole night tossing on her straw mattress and thinking of Snow.

Rapunzel had never known her own father, or her mother, either, for that matter. She had often wondered what it would be like to meet them, but she didn't miss them the way she knew Snow had missed King White. What would it be like to get your father back but not *really* have him back at all?

I'm glad I have Mother Gothel, Rapunzel thought. She and her foster mother had not always had a cozy relationship — it wasn't easy to warm up to a witch. But lately Rapunzel and her "mother" had been getting along great. The old witch had even come to accept that Rapunzel climbed out of her tower every day to attend Princess School. Rapunzel was looking forward to learning more about the witch side of her foster family for the combined Princesses Past and Present and Stitchery project. Creating a family tree sounded like fun — even if she did have to embroider it onto a piece of muslin.

"Finally!" Rapunzel said aloud as she spotted Ella hurrying breathlessly down the path at the same time that Rose was descending from her golden coach.

"Have you heard anything?" Ella called out.

"I was hoping you had," Rapunzel said. "What happened after I left?"

"I departed shortly after you did," Ella explained. "My stepmother was off having supper with the Duke of Ellington, but Hagatha and Prunilla would have tattled for sure if I didn't finish every single one of my chores."

Waving good-bye to the fairies, Rose ran toward the other two. "Have you —"

Rapunzel and Ella shook their heads.

"He still hadn't remembered a thing when I left last night. Maybe a good night's sleep . . ." Rose trailed off. She was looking toward the wood.

Rapunzel turned and saw Snow skipping toward them, holding her father's hand and pulling him along behind her. She looked like her ever-cheerful self.

"Hi-ho!" Snow called. The girls waved and hurried to meet her.

"Good morning," Ella said to Snow and King White. "How are you feeling today?" she asked carefully.

King White smiled kindly. "Much warmer and drier, thank you."

Rapunzel knew Ella was too polite to ask the question they all wanted an answer to. She would have to ask it herself. "Has your memory come back yet?" she blurted.

Rapunzel regretted her bluntness the moment the words were out of her mouth. Snow's pale face fell like a faulty soufflé.

"All Father can remember is his life at sea," Snow explained sadly. "He commanded three ships. They were in an awful storm. Then he woke up on shore. That's all he knows." Snow gripped her father's hand more tightly. "Maybe today . . ."

Rapunzel could tell it was an effort for the poor girl to keep her hopes up.

"I'm not sure how I got here, or where my ships are

now," King White said. "But I feel a good deal better than I did yesterday thanks to Snow and her small friends."

Rapunzel studied King White for a minute. All in all he looked handsome and much more like a king than the near-drowned creature they'd rescued yesterday. He was wearing the clothes they'd found him in, including the blue-and-white striped sailor's cap — not exactly a crown but he wore it well. He still looked dazed and tired, but Snow and the dwarves had done a nice job cleaning him up. His clothes were dry. His hair was cut. In fact his face was cut a little, too. Rapunzel hadn't noticed any cuts yesterday.

Snow saw Rapunzel looking at the small nicks on her father's face and neck. "Wheezer had a bit of a sneezing fit when he was giving Father a shave," she said apologetically.

"I told him I could do it myself but the dwarves are quite strong-willed." King White started to smile, but then yawned. "I beg your pardon," he said to the four princesses.

"Gruff put Father's bed underneath the cuckoo clock, so he's not particularly well rested," Snow explained. She turned to King White and looked up at him. "I'm so sorry, Father."

"Not to worry," King White responded, but Rapunzel thought she saw him wince a little at the word "father."

"You'll never guess where I found him this morning." Snow's smile returned as she waited for her friends to guess.

"Where, Snow?" Ella asked gently.

"The woods!" Snow blurted happily. "He was tending the plants in the woods!"

Rapunzel exchanged a bewildered look with Rose. Did Snow think that was a *good* sign?

"When I couldn't sleep this morning I went outside," King White told them. "The garden was so well cared for, there wasn't much for me to do. So when I got to the edge of the forest I just kept on tending."

"He still has his green thumb!" Snow chirped. "Father used to be ever so good at tending the castle gardens. Malodora sometimes had to scream at him to 'get out of that awful dirt.'"

At least he remembers his hobby, Rapunzel thought. *That is a good sign.*

"Who is Malodora?" King White asked innocently.

Snow gasped.

"Oh, no one important," Rapunzel said, smiling broadly and ushering the whole group toward the school. But her smile was forced — Snow's stepmother had been horrible to both Snow and her husband. How could King White have forgotten *that*?

King White gently touched a rose vine that was

growing up along the edge of the drawbridge. "Lovely roses," he murmured. "But they certainly could use a trim."

Snow leaned in close to her friends. "I brought him back inside as soon as I found him," she whispered. "I didn't dare leave him there alone. I'm so frightened Malodora will find out he is back and curse him again . . . or worse!"

"We'll have to keep his identity a secret," Rose said smartly. "The fewer people who know who he is, the better."

"Poor Father couldn't tell anyone who he is even if he wanted to." Snow gazed at her dad, who was now leaning over the bridge staring longingly at the water below and absentmindedly removing the withered blossoms from the climbing rosebush.

"So, um, what are we going to do with him here at —" The school trumpets interrupted Rapunzel and all of the girls jumped.

"Come on!" Rose called. "We're late!" They hurried inside, pulling Snow's father along with them.

Since princess etiquette was still quite new to her, Rapunzel was not sure which was worse, being late or arriving with an unexpected guest.

Oh, well, she thought with a shrug. They were about to find out.

The other Bloomers were all already in their seats

when Rapunzel stepped into the hearthroom chamber after her friends and King White. Rapunzel almost laughed when she saw the politely bewildered expressions on the faces of the other novice princesses who had just witnessed their breathless entrance. Then her eyes fell on Madame Garabaldi.

Madame Garabaldi hardly ever greeted the girls with a smile, but her scowl seemed especially chiseled this morning.

"You're nearly tardy, all four of you," she said quietly as she looked over their guest. "Or should I say, all five of you." Madame Garabaldi eyed King White with obvious disdain. "Who is this? Is one of you capable of making a proper introduction and explaining this interruption?"

"Begging your pardon, Madame." Snow blushed and curtsied as she spoke. "This is, um . . ." Snow's finger was making its way toward her mouth. Clearly she was not sure what to say.

"Thornbury Green," Rapunzel blurted. "Uh . . . Madame Garabaldi, may I please introduce our new . . . visitor, Sir Thornbury Green. Sir Thornbury, this is our gracious hearthroom teacher, Madame Garabaldi." She made a flourish toward Snow's father and mimed a little bow. Luckily the confused king got the hint and bowed low.

"Oh! Yes! He's the new gardener," Rose said, taking Rapunzel's lead.

"Lady Bathilde asked us to get him acquainted with the castle," Ella added.

"He's going to tend all of the plants and flowers," Snow chimed in, looking relieved. "He's very good at —" Rapunzel stepped lightly on Snow's foot to keep her from babbling, and the pale princess stopped talking.

All of the other Bloomers in their class stared at Ella, Snow, Rapunzel, Rose, and King White. Madame Garabaldi was silent. The instructor looked extremely skeptical.

"Clearly I don't have any flowers to tend in my hearthroom chamber," Madame Garabaldi said sternly.

Snow's father gazed around the large room. "An unfortunate fact," he said, shaking his head sadly, then looking straight into the teacher's eyes. "Perhaps a fresh bouquet from the gardens will repair the oversight. It's a well-known fact that beauty thrives in beauty's presence."

Rapunzel hid her grin. King White was downright charming! "We just dropped in to inform you that we're taking him to the gardens for Lady Bathilde," she said. Then, before Madame Garabaldi could protest, Rapunzel pulled Rose, who pulled Ella, who pulled Snow, who pulled the new gardener out of the chamber.

Chapter Six
Family Tree

Ella stifled a giggle as she followed Rapunzel and Rose down the corridor. Snow and "Thornbury" ambled along behind.

"I can't believe Madame Garabaldi fell for that," Ella whispered.

"It was Rapunzel's clever introduction," Rose replied.

"And everyone else's additions," Rapunzel put in. "But now we need to remember to call him Sir Thornbury when we're on school grounds, so nobody figures out who he really is. And we have to get Sir Thornbury settled in the gardens — before we run into Lady Bathilde!"

"Oh, I hadn't thought of that!" Snow gasped. "Let's hurry!"

Ella grabbed Snow's hand and gave it a reassuring squeeze as Rapunzel picked up the pace and led everyone out of the castle and onto the Princess

School grounds. The group made their way past several statues of famous royals and hedges pruned to look like esteemed Princess School headmistresses of the past. Unfortunately, most of the hedges were so overgrown the headmistresses appeared to have grown blooming beards and birds' nests in their hair.

"My, my," Thornbury clucked disapprovingly.

They made their way to the gardener's shed, where the real Princess School gardener, Jubal Crabgrass, was gathering some tools. He looked up and smiled at the girls as they approached.

"We've brought you some help," Rapunzel announced, gesturing to Thornbury. "Jubal Crabgrass, meet Thornbury Green."

Snow's father gave another low bow. The girls giggled, and Jubal raised an eyebrow in surprise.

"No need for fancy pomp out here," he said, scratching his scraggly salt-and-pepper hair. "You know your way around a rosebush?"

"Indeed," Thornbury replied. "And azaleas and magnolias and fruit trees as well," he said, gesturing to the various plants and trees in the gardens.

Jubal grinned. "Glad to have your help, then," he said. "I've been a bit under the weather, and with the onslaught of rain we've had, I'm a good deal behind." He handed Thornbury a pair of gloves and some shears. Thornbury gave the girls a quick wave, then headed straight for a nearby rosebush and began to prune.

Ella felt a sense of relief. It looked as though they'd be able to leave Thornbury in the gardens without any difficulty. But she wanted to do all she could to make sure he would be safe.

"Thornbury is new to our land, so please keep a close eye on him," she said to Jubal.

"Yes, please do!" Snow agreed. "He tends to wander." Her eyes were wide with worry. Ella put an arm around her friend and gently turned her back toward the castle. Rose and Rapunzel were right beside them.

"He'll be just fine," Rose consoled Snow.

"And isn't it wonderful that he remembers how to garden!" Ella added. "He didn't learn that at sea."

Snow nodded as the Princess School doors whooshed open quietly, welcoming them back into the giant castle foyer. Moments later they were slipping into their seats in the Princesses Past and Present chamber.

At the front of the classroom, Madame Istoria beamed. The petite teacher strode back and forth, waving her arms excitedly.

"Today we will begin to create our royal family trees," she said, gesturing to a tall stack of thick scrolls and leather-bound books piled neatly on her desk. The stack, Ella noticed, was nearly as tall as Madame Istoria herself.

"With special permission, Princess School has borrowed these documents from the Royal Office of Kingdom Records." The teacher stood on her tiptoes and patted the pile of books affectionately. "Valuable information about your families is contained in these documents, and I trust that each and every one of you shall endeavor to search carefully to create your family trees."

Rapunzel leaned across the aisle. "I've already been quizzing Mother Gothel about her family," she whispered to her friends. "Witches are fascinating. For one thing, in a witch family, women do the majority of the magic and make most of the decisions. The warlocks are in charge of brews and cleaning and tending the familiars. It's no wonder Mother Gothel is such a lousy cook!"

"Wow!" Rose said, sounding a little envious. "My family is nowhere near that interesting." She let out a little sigh. "It's stuffy, overprotective, well-bred royals all around. Not a frog in sight. Just a bunch of bossy bluebloods who think they run the kingdom." Then she let out a little giggle. "Though sometimes I think the fairies and servants are the ones really in charge."

"That's better than my household," Ella said with a

grimace. "My stepmother, Kastrid, is definitely in charge, and that's *not* a good thing. I'm going to focus on my father's side of the family for the tree. I want to learn more about his siblings and ancestors. Kastrid hardly ever allows him to talk about them. But if it's homework, she can't object. Maybe I can actually have a conversation with my father!"

Ella glanced over at Snow's pale, sad face and instantly regretted her words. "Oh, Snow," she said. "I'm so sorry. I wasn't thinking of —"

Snow smiled weakly. "It's all right, Ella," she said. "Someday my own father will remember his ancestors, and his offspring." She dabbed at a damp eye, then let out a small sob. "Oh, I feel like my family tree has been chopped down!"

Chapter Seven

Lost and Found

Snow picked up a rose petal and sighed. She was supposed to be working on a flower garland for her hair, the most recent assignment in Looking Glass class. But she was too worried about her father to concentrate. Looking down at her work, she realized that she had just strung half a dozen green leaves together, with nothing colorful in between.

"Oh, dear!" Snow cried softly, quickly unstringing the leaves. "With a garland like that I'll look like an elf, not a princess!"

Beside her, Rose giggled softly. She had already finished her garland and was tying off her thread. She set the circle of flowers on her head and looked in the mirror. "I rather like elves," she said.

Snow smiled. "Me, too," she admitted. "But right now all I can think about is my father. I hope he's all right in the gardens!"

Ella reached over and patted Snow's arm. "I'm sure he's fine," she said. "Jubal is looking after him, remember?"

Just then, as if on cue, the chamber doors swished open and Jubal walked into the room carrying a basket of flower blossoms. "For your garlands," he explained as he set the basket on the carved table at the front of the room.

"At least I thought he was," Ella added quietly.

"Thank you, Jubal," Madame Spiegel said, clearly pleased. Her wide-set brown eyes were shining. "They're just beautiful."

Snow's own eyes were also wide, but not with pleasure. If Jubal was here in the castle, who was looking after her father in the gardens?

Before Snow could gather her thoughts or her skirts to question the gardener, Rapunzel boldly approached him. After several long moments of hushed conversation, Jubal quickly left the chamber, his slightly tattered coattails flapping behind him.

"It's all right," Rapunzel whispered as she walked past Snow's seat toward her own. "Thornbury is still working happily in the rose garden."

Snow let out a small sigh of relief and got back to work on her garland. The new flowers were truly lovely. She strung a tiny purple rosebud for the center and added a few more colorful blooms to the sides. Then she tied off the thread and set the delicate wreath on her head.

Gazing at herself in the mirror, Snow was reminded of the hours and hours she and her father had spent making garlands of apple blossoms in their castle orchard.

"Oh!" Snow cried aloud. How she missed those happy times! She and her father had always had such wonderful fun in the orchard. Seeing the blooms in the mirror brought all those memories flooding back.

I will show Father the garland, Snow thought. *Perhaps it will jog his memory, too.*

As soon as the trumpet sounded, signalling the beginning of lunch, Snow and her friends headed out to the gardens to check on Thornbury. Snow touched the flower garland still in her hair as she scanned the Princess School grounds, hoping to spot him. But though the rose vines over the drawbridge were now neatly trimmed and the headmistress-shaped hedges looked their royal best, Snow's father was nowhere in sight.

"Let's try the rose garden," Rapunzel suggested.

Picking up their skirts, the four girls hurried across the grounds. They were a little out of breath by the time they reached the thorny bushes. Jubal was battling a rather tall rose with a pair of long shears.

"Jubal!" Rose called out.

The gardener was so startled he nearly fell off his ladder. "Oh, hello," he greeted, mopping his brow.

"Jubal," Rapunzel said a bit sternly. "Where is Thornbury?"

A look of embarrassment crossed Jubal's face. "I'm afraid I don't know, Your young Highnesses," he admitted. "These roses pulled me into their overgrown tangle and, uh, I lost track of him. But I'm sure he's close by."

"Oh, no!" Snow cried, covering her face with her hands and knocking off her garland. Ella quickly bent to pick it up and placed it back on Snow's head.

Rapunzel planted a hand on her hip and was about to scold the gardener when Rose pulled her away. "It was an honest mistake, and what's done is done," she said quietly. "We need to find Thornbury. Quickly."

Rapunzel nodded. "Jubal, if you see Thornbury, please ask him to wait here in the rose garden for us." She tried not to sound as irritated as she felt. "And please be sure he does."

Jubal nodded gravely. "I will, m'lady," he vowed.

The girls hurried away and began to search. They checked the gazebo, the fountain, and the stables. They combed the entire garden, and the neighboring Charm School for Boys grounds as well. He was not there.

A faint cackle echoed through the air, and the girls looked up. In the distance a curl of smoke rose out from one of the Grimm School chimneys.

"You don't suppose he could have wandered onto the Grimm School grounds," Ella said, her voice full of horror.

Snow instantly turned as white as a freshly washed sheet. Malodora was headmistress at Grimm.

"Why would he?" Rose asked logically. "There's nothing green there."

"Perhaps he felt that garden needed him even more," Snow said, her voice shaking. "That would be just like Father."

Without another word, the girls lifted their skirts and raced toward the Grimm School. They were in such a rush that Snow almost forgot what a terrifying thing they were doing. Then, as the hideous, smoke-stained castle came into close view, Snow shuddered.

Aside from the colorful and enchanted gingerbread gate, the Grimm School was a dismal sight. Dank, brackish moss covered the outside of the gray stone structure, and the grounds were scorched and barren. Snow had seen it many times since it was between her cottage and Princess School. She had even gone inside when she thought the Grimm witches were harming the woodland animals. But its thoroughly unwelcoming appearance was always a shock, and the knowledge that her horrible stepmother Malodora was inside always made Snow quiver.

The girls approached cautiously, gaping at the menacing rival school.

"Look!" Ella cried, pointing to the gingerbread gate. A tiny piece was missing—it looked as though someone had sampled it!

Everyone knew that the sweet gate of the Grimm School was there to lure in the unwitting.

Snow had a sudden, awful thought — what if her father had forgotten about that, too?

Huddled together, the girls stepped past the gate onto the Grimm School grounds. Snow was grateful that her friends were with her, but even their presence couldn't stop that all-too-familiar icy feeling creeping up the back of her neck — the feeling that Malodora was watching her. The evil witch used to watch Snow constantly in her magic mirror — the one she used to work her terrible magic. Snow feared the mirror almost as much as she feared the queen.

Had the mirror already shown Malodora that Snow's father had returned to shore? Was Malodora fixing to use another curse to send him back to sea? Snow wiped a tear from her cheek. Even if he never regained his memory, Snow could not bear to lose her father again.

With a shiver Snow looked up at a Grimm School tower window. Through the filthy glass she could just make out a tall, shadowy figure peering down at them. The awful witch didn't need her mirror to view Snow now. Snow gasped. "We have to get out of here!" she cried.

"You don't have to tell me twice," Rapunzel agreed. "I'm not afraid of witches, but this place gives me the regal creeps. Besides, I don't think Thorn — I mean, your father — is here."

Tightening their huddle, the girls turned back toward the gate and broke into a run. They ran until they were back on the edge of the Charm School grounds.

"What's that?" Rose pointed toward something caught on the branch of a gnarled tree. It was striped blue and white and hung limply.

"Father's hat!" Snow cried. She grabbed the cap from the limb. "There's something on it," she said, licking her finger. "Frosting!"

"From the gate?" Ella asked, biting her lip.

Snow nodded. "What if . . ."

"He's not at Grimm." Rapunzel looked into Snow's face when she spoke. "Even if he is, we can't go back there now. It's not safe with Malodora watching. We've got to keep moving."

Snow nodded, relieved to let Rapunzel take charge.

The long-haired princess nudged the other girls ahead. Snow felt woozy as she followed her friends across the Charm School grounds.

Suddenly they heard a muffled cry.

"Did you hear that?" Ella asked.

The others nodded. "I think it came from in there," Rose said. She pointed to the Charm School's huge labyrinth hedge. It was taller than a stack of twenty mattresses and covered an area nearly as large as a jousting arena.

Snow pointed to the corner near the entrance. It had recently been pruned into the shape of a sailing vessel.

"Father!" Snow gulped. There was relief in her voice. "Father!" she called, more loudly. "Can you hear me?" They heard another muffled, indiscernible cry. "He's in the labyrinth!" Snow confirmed. "Thank goodness."

"We still have to find him," Rapunzel said sensibly. "I've been in there before, with Val. There's no danger except in the center, but it's royally easy to get lost." She tapped her slippered foot on the paving stones thoughtfully. Then she grinned and raised a finger in the air. "I have an idea." She quickly unraveled her braid, coiling it on her arm. Then she tied the end to a hedge branch at the entrance to the labyrinth. "This will keep us from getting lost," she said. "We'll be all right as long as we stick together." Holding hands and letting out Rapunzel's hair as they went, the girls made their way into the labyrinth.

"This is amazing," Rose whispered as she led the group forward on the puzzle path. Her blue eyes were bright with excitement.

Ella shivered. "Too many twists and turns for me," she said. "Thank crowns for your hair, Rapunzel. Getting lost in here would be almost as bad as getting lost on the Grimm School grounds."

"Is someone there?" a muffled voice called.

"We're coming, Father!" Snow cried. "Just stay where you are!"

Luckily, Thornbury had done a bit of trimming along the way. The girls passed ships of all kinds. Still, they took several wrong turns. Finally, the girls found Thornbury sitting inside the puzzle, leaning against a hedge wall looking tired and confused.

"Oh, Father!" Snow cried, rushing up to him. "We were so worried about you! Whatever are you doing in the labyrinth?"

"You're lucky you didn't get all the way to the Minotaur in the center," Rapunzel told him. "He despises visitors."

Snow clung to her father, tears of relief washing down her pale face. The floral garland sat askew on her raven hair. "You shan't leave the Princess School grounds again. Or go anywhere near that awful Grimm School," she wailed. "Malodora works there, and there's no telling what she would do if she found you, Father."

"Malodora?" King White repeated blankly. "Didn't someone mention her this morning? I'm certain I know no one of that name. And someone I've never met can't bear me a grudge." He looked kindly at Snow. "Please, dear child, do not call me Father. For though you are most certainly the sweetest daughter a man could have, I am not able to call you mine." He gently straightened the garland on Snow's head.

Snow looked up at her father in disbelief. "I must call you something." Her voice was almost a whisper. "Uncle, then," she said more strongly, though her eyes were brimming with tears. "I will call you Uncle Thornbury."

Snow's father smiled and patted Snow on the head. "Uncle it is," he agreed.

Chapter Eight

Back the Way You Came

Rose was filled with mixed emotions as she and the others followed Rapunzel's hair out of the labyrinth and made their way back to the Princess School gardens. Relief that they'd found Snow's father. Disappointment that he still had no idea who he was. Worry that he was clearly still cursed by Malodora. And empathy for her sweet friend Snow, who was obviously filled with sadness — and worry.

"Please, Uncle," Snow said for the fifth time. "You mustn't wander. It simply isn't safe!"

Thornbury smiled at Snow. "Your concern for me is very sweet," he said. "But I wish you wouldn't fret so. You've already been so kind to a washed-up stranger. Don't burden yourself with thoughts for my well-being."

Rose saw Snow's face fall, and her heart went out to her. Sometimes Rose's dad drove her to the edge of a castle tower, but at least he knew who she was.

"This stone wall and the scrolled gates mark the edge of the Princess School grounds," Rose told Thornbury. "And with all these overgrown flowers and shrubs, you and Jubal should have plenty to do. No need to go trimming at other schools."

"We don't want you to feel fenced in, but we would all be less worried if you would stay on Princess School grounds," Rapunzel added.

"Look, there's Jubal!" Ella said, pointing ahead.

Jubal was still up on his ladder tangled in the same giant rosebush, muttering something about the vine having a mind of its own.

Rapunzel picked a second pair of shears off the ground and handed them to Snow's father. "I think Jubal could use some help," she said with a giggle. "He doesn't seem to be making much progress on his own."

"Indeed," Thornbury agreed. He pulled on his gloves and approached the bramble from the other side, a look of determination on his face.

"Uncle —"

Thornbury held up his hand. "Dear Snow," he said. "I will not leave the Princess School grounds again. I promise."

"Thank you," Snow replied, heaving a sigh of relief.

"We'd better get to class," Rose said, quickly picking a few apples from a nearby tree and handing them out. "We're late as it is."

"I'm so sorry!" Snow told her friends. "I didn't mean to get anyone in trouble!"

"Don't be silly, Snow," Ella said, patting her friend's arm. "We're all in this together."

Waving good-bye, the girls hurried across the lawns to the castle. But before they even got close to the shining marble stairs they saw Madame Garabaldi walking toward them.

"What should we do?" Snow cried.

"Let me do the talking," Rose said. "I'm sure I can come up with something."

At least I hope I can, she thought, racking her brain for a way to avoid a lecture about being late and unkempt, and wandering out of the castle between classes.

Rose stepped up to her hearthroom teacher, smiled sweetly, and gave a little curtsy. Behind her, her friends did the same.

"What is this?" Madame Garabaldi asked sternly. Her silver-streaked hair was pulled so tightly into its bun that Rose wondered if she could close her eyes all the way.

"Well, you see, madame," Rose began slowly, stalling for time while she tried to think of a worthwhile excuse, "we were just, um . . ."

Rose gazed up at the teacher to gauge her expression, and noticed for the first time that Madame

Garabaldi was looking behind them instead of at them, and she appeared to be . . . smiling.

Rose looked over her shoulder and saw Snow's father coming after them. In his arms was a giant bouquet of roses.

"How lovely to see you again, madame," he said with a slow bow.

Rose hid a smile behind her hand. Not only was Thornbury rescuing them from the wrath of Madame G., he was trying to charm her as well! Too bad, Rose realized, succeeding would be practically impossible. Madame Garabaldi was all royal business.

Thornbury handed over the roses, which had been wrapped in burlap so as not to prick their recipient. "For your classroom, madame," he explained. "Beauty loves company, does it not?"

Madame Garabaldi awkwardly took the roses. "I . . . well, I . . ."

Rose saw that her friends were trying not to giggle. She knew why. None of them had ever seen Madame Garabaldi like this. She was speechless!

Rose couldn't tell if the teacher was pleased or furious. After an awkward moment of silence, Thornbury excused himself and made his way back to the rose garden and Jubal.

Madame Garabaldi stared after him, a dazed expression on her face. "How strange," she said distantly. "I seem to have forgotten where I was going and what I was going there to do. I believe I'll have to go back where I started from and see if it comes to me."

The girls watched as Madame Garabaldi turned and ambled back the way she came, with her arms full of flowers, completely oblivious to them. She was just disappearing behind a statue of an important princess when Snow gasped.

"That's it!" she cried. "I have to take Father back, too."

"Back to hearthroom?" Rapunzel asked.

Rose and Ella looked at each other and shrugged. They didn't understand what Snow meant, either.

"No. Father needs to go back to a place that he knew before he forgot." Snow clapped her hands together. "The orchard!" she exclaimed. Then her excitement turned to horror.

Snow shuddered and hugged herself. She took a deep breath. "I have to take him to Malodora's castle," she whispered.

Chapter Nine
A Terrifying Encounter

Snow awoke the next morning with fear in her heart. She had not been to her father's castle in a very long time.

When Snow and her father had lived together in the castle, it was her favorite place in the world. Snow's happiest memories were of long afternoons spent playing in the apple orchard with her father. But then King White had married Malodora. The castle became darker and gloomier almost immediately, and then, out of the blue, Snow's father disappeared. One glimpse in Malodora's magic mirror had confirmed Snow's most terrifying nightmare: her father was lost at sea in a terrible, never-ending storm, cursed by his own wife.

Snow had fled to the dwarves' cottage and had not returned. She sensed that Malodora guarded the castle as a lion guards a fresh kill, and that she would be equally fierce with an intruder. Snow's blissful memories were all she had to keep her hopes alive. Seeing what Malodora had done to the castle might destroy those hopes forever.

Snow did her best not to let her worries show at breakfast. She even managed to eat a bowl of oatmeal and raspberries and join in as the dwarves sang their favorite breakfast song. But her heart was not in it.

"Father and I," she began, then paused. "*Uncle* and I are going for a walk in the forest this morning," she told the dwarves as she cleared her bowl. She hated misleading them, but she didn't want them to worry. At the moment she was worrying enough for all eight of them, and she knew this was something she and her father needed to take care of themselves.

"Fine," Gruff huffed as he snatched King White's bowl away from the table and carried it to the sink. Snow's father looked up in surprise. He had not yet eaten his last bite.

"Be gone with you, then," Gruff muttered, brushing past Snow without offering his bristly cheek for a good-bye kiss.

The dwarves had not been particularly friendly around her father lately, Snow noticed. But she did not have time to think about it.

"Come, Uncle," Snow said as cheerfully as she

could. "There's something I'd like you to see." She handed him his coat and hat and led him outside.

Snow forced herself to hum a cheerful little tune as they made their way through the forest. The path to Malodora's castle was dark with overgrown branches that blocked the light, and thick tree roots marred the earth.

"Where are we going?" King White asked.

"To a ruined castle," Snow said quickly, wiping a tear from her cheek. "It was once a sparkling paradise, but now it's nothing but a place of darkness and evil."

King White frowned. "I don't understand," he said. "Why would you want to go there?"

Snow sighed, feeling a heaviness in her chest. "In truth, I don't," she admitted. "But we aren't going inside. We are going to the gardens."

A little flicker sparkled in Snow's heart. Secretly she held out hope that the gardens would only be neglected and not ruined. "It's your old garden, Fa — Uncle. Our old garden. And I am hoping that seeing it will spark your memory." Snow felt the flicker within her glow into an ember. She fanned the flame of hope, imagining the look on her father's face when he remembered everything. She only prayed he would not be too upset by the awful changes Malodora had made to their old home. Stopping, she took her father's hand. "You must promise you will not despair when you see what an awful place Malodora has turned your castle into."

King White smiled kindly. "Dear Snow," he said, "I am quite sure the castle was never mine, so I can feel no attachment to it."

Snow felt her heart sink in her chest at these words, but she did not reply. It was no use arguing with her father. He simply didn't remember who he was.

Snow pulled her father's hand and led him the last hundred yards up the path to the castle. She didn't dare look at the blackened towers of her former home. If Malodora was watching them, Snow didn't want to know. She was going to bring her father to the orchard no matter what. She steeled herself for her first view of the orchards. Would the trees be budding? Bearing fruit? She could not wait to see. But when they stepped around the east tower into the clearing, Snow and her father stopped short and stared, agape, at the horrible sight.

The once lush and fruit-laden trees were gone, with nothing but blackened stumps to show where they formerly stood. Here and there the ground still smoldered. Every living thing had been burned down.

Snow watched her father gaze sadly and confusedly around him. She searched his face for some sign of recognition. When she saw none, her heart sank even further.

"You recognize . . . nothing?" she asked sadly, already knowing the answer.

Because in truth she did not recognize anything, either. This was not the orchard of her memories — of either of their memories. How could this blackened, stump-ridden place trigger happy recollections?

Snow looked down sadly. Smoke rose from the still-warm ashes near her feet. Snow suddenly realized the sickening truth: Malodora had burned the orchard only recently. She must have known they were coming.

Slam! Snow spun back toward the castle to see a dark figure emerging from the castle's south entrance. Malodora.

Snow stepped forward and took her father's hand without thinking. Malodora strode toward them, her dark purple robes fluttering behind her and her haunting face contorted into a furious scowl.

"How dare you trespass on my property," she hissed, glaring at Snow. The poor girl did not dare mention that the property still belonged to them.

The queen's eyes darted from Snow to her father and back. "I thought you might come snooping around here." Malodora squinted into the sun. "I took the liberty of trimming the trees for you." She laughed cruelly. "Or maybe you came back to see me," the haughty evil queen demurred, batting her long dark lashes. She was truly beautiful, but so cold. Snow clutched her father's hand more tightly.

Malodora looked up at the pair through lowered lids. Then her expression shifted. She looked amused . . . and evil. "Or did you come to ask for another spell? A more permanent one, perhaps?" She pointed a long finger at her husband. "I'm certain I could come up with something a little more lethal this time."

Snow shuddered and took a step closer to her father. His face had suddenly paled. Did he recognize the evil witch standing before them? He seemed to know enough to fear her. Did Malodora know his memory was still gone? Snow was suddenly filled with terror. She should never have brought her father here! What if the awful witch made things worse?

Malodora's fists balled at her sides. She locked her eyes on her husband. "This foolish girl's all-conquering love brought you back, no doubt," she sneered. Then Malodora leaned close to Snow's ear. "Take heed, stupid child. My curse has not been lifted entirely. Though his body has returned to you, his mind remains at sea, aimlessly wandering the waves. His memory is adrift, my dear, where I intend to keep it. Forever. Your simpering love cannot restore his mind." She raised her arms into the air, laughing, and a blinding streak of lightning cracked the sky.

"Please," Snow begged, dropping to her knees on the blackened soil. "He means nothing to you. Lift the curse. Let him come back to me!"

Malodora threw her head back with an evilly glee-ful cackle. "Never!" she cried. "I will never unlock his memory, nor reveal the secret of the spell."

Her light blue eyes bored into Snow's dark ones, sending a shocking chill right through her.

"Now, be gone with you," she screeched. "Before your sweetness makes something . . . flourish!"

Snow shakily got to her feet. Taking her dazed father by the elbow, she began to lead him away. As they neared the edge of the forest, he stopped to pick up a singed stick. It was the broken branch of an apple tree — the only one that was not completely burnt.

Tears streamed down Snow's face as she led her bewildered father back to the cottage. Her whole body felt weak. Just seeing Malodora had sucked the strength right out of her. If she weren't responsible for her father she would not have found the strength to make it home — she was too overcome with help-lessness.

Oh, Snow, you selfish girl! she scolded herself. *At least* you *have your memories*. All her father had was the bare branch of an apple tree from a castle he had no memory of ruling.

"What an awful woman," Snow's father finally

remarked as she weakly pulled him down the lane. "I've never met anyone so terrible. And those gardens. Why isn't anything growing there? The light is good. . . ."

He trailed off, deep in thought about the orchard. Snow's heart practically fell to her feet. Her father's mind really was out to sea.

Chapter Ten

Up a Tree

Rapunzel slouched unroyally over her desk, alone in the Princesses Past and Present chamber. It was the end of lunch period, and she'd eaten in a hurry so she'd have time to work on her family tree. Dipping her quill in ink, she quickly blotted it and wrote furiously. What was it Mother Gothel had said about her sister's children? She knew there were twin warlocks in the family, but she'd muttered something else about a white sheep. Was there a daughter, too? Rapunzel would have to ask Mother Gothel again tonight. For days Rapunzel had been hearing stories about her foster family. They were better than fairy tales! And she had discovered some very interesting twists.

Rapunzel drew a branch on her parchment with three forks and left one of them blank. There. She sat back to admire the spooky family tree. It was large, gnarled, and lopsided — just like the giant old oak by her tower. Rapunzel thought it was perfect. But she had more work to do.

Unrolling a fresh scroll, Rapunzel began her real family tree. She'd decided to do two. After all, she did have two families. And besides, her "real" tree did not take long to draw. With just one dip of her quill she was done. Two sets of grandparents. Two parents. One Rapunzel. No aunts. No uncles. No cousins. And her parents and grandparents weren't around anymore. The tree looked weak and spindly, not nearly as impressive as her witch tree.

Looking up, Rapunzel saw that the rest of the Bloomers were beginning to arrive. She scanned the coiffed heads, looking for her friends. They hadn't had a moment to talk all day and she could not wait to tell them the incredible tidbit she'd learned last night. Turning back to her Gothel tree, Rapunzel added a flourish to the name on one of the larger roots: Great-great-grandmother Gertrudis Grimm, as in Grimm School for Witches. Rapunzel could not believe it when Mother Gothel told her it was Gertrudis and her brothers who started the school generations ago. But the really shocking part was that Mother Gothel was not a Grimm graduate. She had been kicked out!

"Bat's breath!" Mother Gothel had screeched after she'd confessed her unplanned departure to Rapunzel. "All of those rules. Who could break them all? The old bats running that place were stiffer than Granny's lockjaw."

Giggling to herself, Rapunzel scanned for the flaxen heads of Ella and Rose as well as Snow's raven one. When she finally spotted them the giggle died on her lips. Ella and Rose were huddled around Snow, obviously trying to cheer her up. Rapunzel quickly left her high-backed chair and poked her own braid-wrapped head into the mix. "No luck in the orchard?" she asked.

One look at Snow and she knew she hadn't even needed to ask. Snow had obviously been crying. And the rash around her mouth could only mean one thing: She'd been eating entirely too much applesauce.

Madame Istoria rapped her scepter on the pile of books at the front of the room to call the class to order.

"We're going to meet at Snow's house after school," Rose said in a whisper. "Don't worry, Snow. We'll come up with a new plan." Ella and Rapunzel patted Snow on the shoulder. She was so downcast she looked like she was melting, but she managed a small smile.

The day dragged on like a taffeta train on the longest of red carpets. Rapunzel felt it would never end. She was so intent on listening for the final trumpet blast that when it finally sounded she jumped. At last!

You'd think after being locked up for so many years I

might have a little patience, Rapunzel thought. But the opposite was true. After too many years in her tower Rapunzel was ready to go. If there was a problem or task to tackle, she hated having to wait. She would rather jump in and get things done, set a game plan, and charge!

"Let's go get Thorny and put our heads together." Rapunzel clapped her hands in the hall.

"I do hope he's okay," Snow fretted.

"Of course he is. Jubal wouldn't let him wander off twice," Rapunzel reassured her friend.

But when she, Rose, Ella, and Snow reached the peony beds Jubal was working alone.

"Where is he?" Ella gasped.

"Who?" Jubal mopped his brow absently. His salt-and-pepper hair stood up in all directions. Then, noticing the looks of horror on the faces of the four princesses, he stood straighter. "You must mean Thornbury!" He slapped his forehead. "Of course. Why, he's been gone for hours. He mentioned something about the flowers needing fertilizer. I thought he was headed to the barn, but . . ." The gardener's voice trailed off.

"Hours," Snow moaned, sinking to the ground.

"Terribly sorry." Jubal wrung his hands.

"He could be anywhere," Snow said quietly.

Ella and Rose dropped down beside her.

"Or, he could be right here." Rapunzel pointed toward a tall man walking up behind them. His face was hidden behind the huge bundle he was carrying and he smelled strongly of the ocean.

"Seaweed!" Thornbury said, dropping his load. Slippery green tendrils spilled out of a giant burlap sack. "It's just what these plants are wanting. It's rich in minerals," he said, spreading the slimy stuff around the base of the peonies. "And it gave me a good excuse to visit the shore."

Pushing up her sleeves, Rapunzel began to help spread the seaweed around the garden. It was clear Thornbury wasn't going to leave until he finished the job. The girls couldn't go home without him, and they needed time back at the cottage to plan. Ignoring the fact that they were not dressed for gardening, Ella, Rose, and Snow dropped to their knees and got to work, too.

"What comfort the sea brings!" Thornbury exclaimed, pulling a large armful of seaweed from the sack.

Rapunzel stole a look at Snow under the jasmine vine. She wished Thornbury would stop talking about the ocean, but he didn't seem to be able to help himself.

"Breathing in the salty air is tonic for my soul. Sometimes I swear I can hear the waves calling me. But," he said more quietly, "when I was sailing something else used to call to me. It was the sweetest voice, and it spoke directly to my heart. Sometimes I still hear it in my dreams."

Rapunzel could hardly believe her ears. He had to be talking about Snow!

"Fath — I mean Uncle, come, it's time to go home," Snow called from a few bushes away. She had not heard what he was saying, and Rapunzel did not want to tell her. It would probably have given her hope, and Rapunzel wasn't sure the poor girl could survive having her hope dashed yet again. For now Snow's father was adrift — and a boat without a keel seldom made it safely to land.

Chapter Eleven
Budding Plan

Rose looked down at her muddy hands and seaweed-stained frock and grinned. Sometimes being a mess was just so . . . fun! Especially when her fairies weren't around to fuss about it. And tonight they had grudgingly agreed to let her go back to Snow's cottage without them. Unfortunately, she and Ella and Rapunzel were not going to Snow's for a friendly visit. They had some serious thinking to do.

Ahead of Rose on the woodland path, Snow walked without humming. Some of her animal friends heard her light footsteps and poked their heads out of their nests and burrows. No doubt they were waiting for the treats and pats and kind words Snow always offered. But today they were disappointed. Rose knew Snow was so worried about Malodora and her father she could think of nothing else.

Ella patted a few squirrels. "She'll be okay," she whispered to them. Rose hoped Ella was right.

When they got to the cottage, several of the dwarves were outside doing chores. Hap chopped wood while Dim and Wheezer loaded the wheelbarrow. Gruff was fetching water from the well. Thornbury gestured to the few tendrils of seaweed still in his burlap sack.

"I do believe I'll give this to the azaleas," he announced. He whistled a sea tune as he rounded the cottage.

"I'll keep an eye on him," Wheezer sniffed, ambling along behind the tall sailor. Snow smiled gratefully. She greeted the rest of the dwarves, and motioned the girls inside.

When they were all seated around the low wooden table, Snow told them all about the visit to the orchard. When she finished there was a long silence. Rose knew they each wished they had an idea to help Snow and her father. But her own mind was a blank.

"What's that?" Rapunzel asked, pointing at a stick poking out of a glass of water on the table. The end of the stick was black, but where it forked the bark was still brown. "Some kind of flower?"

"It's all that's left of our orchard," Snow said, biting her lip to keep it from quivering. "Father picked it up. I'm not sure why I kept it. I mean, it can't possibly grow. The entire orchard was completely charred." A single tear fell onto Snow's pale cheek. She ran a slender finger along the bark, then paused and drew in a sharp breath. "I thought I felt a bump, like a tiny bud just forming." She inspected the branch, then sat back with a sigh. "But it was only wishful thinking."

Rose smiled reassuringly. "You do have a green thumb," she said.

"Just make sure it doesn't grow into a giant beanstalk," Rapunzel added with a grin.

Rose smiled, too, remembering Snow's magic beans. The four friends had gotten themselves into some pretty sticky situations. Working together, they had gotten out of all of them. Rose hoped they would be able to get Snow out of this situation, too. But given a choice, she'd take magic beans and a nasty giant over Malodora.

"I'm so sorry to be so dour," Snow apologized as she stood up to dish out applesauce and pour berry punch. "If you'd only seen Malodora's face when she said she'd never lift the curse." Snow choked on a tiny sob, and Rose reached a hand out to calm her. "It was terrible! And the worst part is, I know something is brewing — she has some nasty trick up her sleeve. Now that she knows Father is back I think she might be planning a new curse!"

"How revolting!" Ella exclaimed. Rose thought she was talking about Malodora, but Ella was focused over Rose's shoulder. Thornbury had just come in behind her, and he was covered in slop!

"Oh, no!" Snow jumped up and began to clean fruit peels from Thornbury's arms.

"It's nothing." Thornbury shrugged, sending a shower of vegetable peels slithering to the floor. "Dim was just dumping out the compost bucket. I guess he didn't see me there under the azaleas."

Rose stifled a laugh. The dwarves were always so sweet and thoughtful, but they certainly seemed to be having a lot of accidents around Snow's father.

"I'll just go clean up." Thornbury ducked upstairs, being careful not to knock his bruised forehead on the low beam.

"Back to Malodora." Rapunzel tapped the table.

"There must be a way to stop her," Ella said, biting her lip.

"I wish Lurlina wasn't on vacation," Ella lamented. "My fairy godmother's timing could use a little work."

"Is there something my fairies can help with?" Rose asked. Before Snow shook her head Rose knew that was a bad idea. The fairies would never allow Rose to dabble in anything dangerous.

Rose shivered, thinking about Malodora and her

large, enchanted, cracked looking glass. Malodora used the mirror to work her dark magic. Rose had seen it herself at the Princess School versus Grimm School Maiden Games, and had no desire to see it ever again.

Rapunzel sighed. "Mother Gothel is powerful, but I'm not sure she could lift a curse —"

"Oh, no!" Snow exclaimed. "Thank you all so much, but I wouldn't want Lurlina or the fairies or Mother Gothel to get mixed up in this. It's too dangerous!"

Snow rested her chin in her hands. "Oh, this is awful! How can we possibly fight magic without magic?"

"We just will." Rapunzel brought her fist down, knocking her applesauce spoon and splattering the table.

"We have to," Rose agreed, licking some stray sauce from the back of her hand.

Ella cleared her throat. "And I think I know what we need to do first. We have to get that mirror."

"Break into the castle?" Snow's voice was a whisper. All four girls stared at one another in silence.

They all knew that the mirror was the main source of Malodora's power. Without it, her spells and curses would be far less powerful — maybe even nonexistent.

"Do you know how to get in, Snow?" Rose put an arm around her friend's shoulders.

Snow shuddered and nodded at the same time, then shoveled a last bite of applesauce into her mouth and gulped it down. Still looking at one another, the girls locked hands.

"I'll do it for Father," Snow said softly.

"We'll do it together," Rose confirmed.

Chapter Twelve
Common Threads

Ella shivered with emotion as she entered the hearthroom chamber. There was too much to think about! Tonight was the night of the castle break-in. She still couldn't believe they were going to try to steal Malodora's magic mirror. If they were caught, Malodora's rage would no doubt make Ella's stepmother Kastrid's fury seem like a walk in the forest. Ella forced the awful thought from her head. They would *not* get caught.

Ella shoved her heavy sewing basket under her polished hearthroom desk. Today was the day they were going to start sewing their family trees in Stitchery and she could not wait. Glancing around the room, Ella was surprised not to see her friends. They hadn't been on the bridge when she'd come across, either. She was eager to tell them what she'd learned about her family the night before.

Pulling out her basket, she pondered colors while

she waited. She could hardly keep the smile from her face. It had been so wonderful sitting in the parlor last night talking with her father after leaving Snow's cottage. Her stepmother had gone out, and Ella and her father had sat in front of the fire with steaming cups of tea and a plate of cookies. Even the glares of her stepsisters had not ruined the evening.

During the conversation, Ella had asked her father what made him decide to marry Kastrid after his first wife, Ella's mother, had died. Ella could not have been more shocked by his answer. "I wanted to make sure you would have opportunities, my dear," he'd said. "Kastrid is an important woman in royal society."

This part of the story Ella already knew, but she didn't have the heart to tell him she'd have had more opportunities had he married a beggar woman. But then, Ella's father went on to explain that there was another reason he had chosen Kastrid as his wife. Kastrid, he said, had lost her own mother when she was just a baby. "She was an orphan, you know," Ella's father said. "So I thought she would take pity on my darling motherless girl."

Ella had almost dropped her teacup in surprise. Kastrid was an orphan? "Perhaps her life was too hard," her father had continued. "Her adoptive family was the wealthiest in five kingdoms, but they treated her horribly."

All Ella could do was stare at her father with her mouth agape while he elaborated. There was no doubt *something* had made Kastrid a bitter person, but Ella had never heard this about her before. For a moment Ella felt terrible for her stepmother. Then she felt angry. How could the woman be so cruel when she knew just what it felt like to be on the receiving end of that cruelty?

I will never be like that, Ella vowed as she chose a brown thread for the trunk of her family tree. She gazed around the nearly-empty hearthroom. Where was everyone?

Just then the door whooshed open and Snow hurried inside, followed by Rapunzel and Rose. Unfortunately Madame Garabaldi was right behind them, and the trumpet was sounding. The girls only had time to wave before they rushed to their high-backed seats for scroll call. Ella would have to tell them her tale later.

Shoving her family tree back in her basket, Ella noticed that her friends all looked nervous and a little tired. No wonder her friends were late. They had probably tossed and turned and not gotten any sleep. Ella had slept poorly, too, knowing that the next night she and her friends would be sneaking into Malodora's castle to steal the magic mirror.

Ella tried to smile reassuringly at Snow. In spite of

her fears, she knew they could do it and wanted Snow to know, too.

At the front of the room, Madame G. called the girls' names in order. Ella was shaken from her thoughts when her own name was called.

"Present," she answered, looking up. Ella blinked in surprise, and stared. Madame Garabaldi did not resemble herself. For one thing, she was wearing a lovely golden yellow gown instead of her usual drab olive or pewter gray. For another, her tight bun was looser today and softened by two small ringlets hanging on either side of her face. And the instructor was actually smiling. Her regal composure was much more relaxed than usual. Ella felt a smile spread across her own face.

"What is the meaning of your ungainly grin?" Madame Garabaldi asked. Her smile vanished.

With an unprincesslike gulp, Ella searched for something to say. "I was just thinking that you look very . . . pretty today, madame."

"Pretty?" Madame Garabaldi repeated, as if she had never heard the word before. Ella felt sure she had said something wrong and waited for the lecture she knew was coming. Luckily, at that moment the classroom door whooshed open and a page came into the chamber, followed by a gentleman carrying a large silver pitcher. It was Thornbury!

"Please pardon the disturbance. I've brought a drink for your roses." The gardener bowed.

The whole room buzzed at Thornbury's arrival. All of the girls smiled at this interruption. Even Snow managed a small grin. Ella knew she was probably just glad to see that her father hadn't wandered off anywhere yet this morning. But that wasn't what the other Bloomers were noticing. Madame Garabaldi was smiling demurely, and her cheeks had turned an exquisite shade of pink.

Only Snow's father seemed not to notice Madame G.'s flushing face. He trotted quickly across the room, refilled the vase on the instructor's desk, and exited again with a bow.

"Oh, where was I?" Madame Garabaldi asked when the door closed behind him. "You are all in attendance, is that correct? I'm sure you are," she said, dropping the scroll she'd been holding onto her desk. The page beside her handed over the next scroll of school announcements. Madame Garabaldi put a handkerchief to her temple and looked toward the high windows. The Bloomers all waited for her to speak. "Since it looks so warm outside, I think we might have today's announcements in the garden," she finally said, sounding a bit dazed. Without uttering another word, Madame Garabaldi smoothed her bun and walked out of the room.

Ella and Rapunzel exchanged looks. The rest of the Bloomers looked at each other, too. Was Madame Garabaldi okay? It wasn't *that* warm, and Madame G. never changed her routine. But Ella was glad for the chance to walk near her friends down the corridor and outside.

The Bloomers whispered among themselves as they hurried after their teacher. "Finally," Rose said. "A chance to talk. How are you doing, Snow?"

Snow blinked rapidly and shrugged. Obviously she was not doing very well.

"It will all be over soon," Rapunzel said, giving Snow's arm a squeeze. She sounded almost excited.

Ella wished for a moment that she shared Rapunzel's taste for adventure. "So, what time are we snatching that horrid looking glass?" she asked, trying to sound confident.

Taking a deep breath, Snow whispered, "Malodora stays up late working on her spells — sometimes for half the night. Then she goes to bed and sleeps like a log. The servants used to come out of her room scalded if they took her tea in too early. She gets just furious if she's awakened. I mean, more furious than normal."

Ella knew all about waking up furious stepmothers too early with the tea tray, but she knew she hadn't seen anything like Malodora's wrath . . . yet.

The girls made their way past the statues and several hedges that had been newly trimmed into the shapes of seafaring ships. Up ahead, Madame Garabaldi had stopped near the rose garden and was motioning for the Bloomers to gather around.

"I think we should go just before sunup tomorrow morning, then," Rapunzel whispered quickly. "Sound okay, Snow?"

Snow nodded slowly, her eyes wide.

"All right," Rapunzel went on. "Snow, I'll meet you at your cottage. Ella, Rose, you two wait for us at the fork in the forest path near the castle. We'll all go in together."

"Right," Ella agreed. She sat down on the ground with the other Bloomers and spread out the skirt of her gown on the manicured lawn. Rapunzel, Rose, and Snow looked anxious as they did the same. Madame Garabaldi looked a bit nervous herself as she prepared to continue with the announcements. She had chosen a spot quite close to the bush Thornbury was trimming.

"Isn't it nice to be out of the classroom?" Madame Garabaldi cooed. "I should teach under this azalea more often!"

"Begging your pardon, madame," Thornbury said, quietly interrupting. "But you are teaching under a rhododendron."

Madame Garabaldi was silent. The entire class

took a collective breath and held it. They knew there was nothing the hearthroom instructor hated more than being corrected. Ella closed her eyes and waited for Thornbury to receive the inevitable tongue-lashing.

"Why, Sir Thornbury, your floral knowledge is quite impressive, and your conduct is so much more stately than that of our regular gardener," Madame Garabaldi replied. "Do you hail from a royal gardening family?"

Ella could not believe her ears. Instead of the acid response the whole class had been expecting, Madame Garabaldi was gushing compliments!

"I am hardly royalty, though some of your students have insisted I must be so," Thornbury said, winking at Snow. "But I do pride myself on knowing a few things about blooms. Flowers and the sea are indeed the only two things I seem to know much about."

"Then perhaps you would be so gracious as to enlighten us on a few more names of the wonderful blossoms in your garden?" Madame G. replied.

Out of the corner of her eye Ella saw Rapunzel bite her lip to keep from laughing out loud. Ella's own hand flew to her mouth to stifle a giggle. Madame Garabaldi was acting like a princess at her first ball! Even Snow was grinning as she leaned closer to Ella.

"Did you hear that?" Snow was whispering, but the excitement in her voice was clear. "Madame G. can tell that my father is a king!"

Chapter Thirteen
Shattered Spell

"Over here," Rapunzel called softly. She stood in a small pool of yellow light.

Snow waved and put her finger to her lips. Then she closed the door to the cottage as silently as possible. The last thing she wanted was to wake the dwarves and worry them or put them in danger, too. It was enough that Malodora had it in for her and her father, and that Snow was about to put Ella, Rapunzel, and Rose in the evil woman's path.

Rapunzel held her lantern a little higher as Snow padded over. Snow noticed that Rapunzel was wearing a charcoal-gray gown, and wished for the first time that she owned a gown that wasn't a bright, cheerful color. Blending into the night was a little trickier in egg-yolk yellow.

"Ready?" Rapunzel asked quietly.

Snow knew she would never in a million years feel ready to reenter the castle that had once been her home. But she also knew she had to do all she could to keep her father safe now that she'd found him again. Besides, her friends would all be there to help her feel brave. And there was no time like the present.

Snow and Rapunzel walked softly through the woods. Now and then Snow heard an owl whoot-whooing his encouragement. Then, suddenly, she heard a different sound.

"Is that them?" Snow heard Ella's voice before she saw her.

"It better be," Rose replied. "I don't think I want to meet anyone else in these woods tonight."

"It's us." Rapunzel held the lantern higher so Rose and Ella could see their faces. The girls were standing at the fork in the path just as they'd planned. Even in the near-darkness Snow could see that her friends' eyes were all wider than usual. And their breathing was a bit scattered. Holding hands, they started down the narrow trail toward the enchanted castle.

"I can't believe we're doing this." Ella's voice sounded shivery in the darkness.

"You don't have to come with —" Snow started to say.

Suddenly a twig snapped. Rose screeched. Ella yanked Snow's hand. Rapunzel plowed into Snow's back, nearly upsetting the lantern.

"Of course we have to come with you!" Rapunzel

said hotly. "And we're going to have to maintain a bit of composure if we expect to do any good." Rapunzel held her lantern up so she could see her friends' faces. She gave them a look Snow remembered from when Rapunzel was a coach at the Maiden Games — her pep-talk look. "Don't let some old mirror and an uptight witch spook you," Rapunzel said. "After all, there are four of us."

Rapunzel's confidence might have been mostly bravado, but it made Snow feel much better. She walked closer to the light and her long-haired friend the rest of the way, feeling her own confidence grow with each quiet step.

When they emerged from the forest Snow could just make out the dim outline of the castle against the sky. The shape was so familiar. In the dark it still looked like her old home. But as a cloud passed out from in front of the slim fingernail of moon and more light shone on the structure, Snow's confidence disappeared.

"She *lives* in there?" Ella stared at the filthy windows and dark-stained castle walls.

"No wonder she feels at home at the Grimm School," Rose added.

Snow nodded sadly. "It used to be beautiful. I wish you could have seen it." Snow led the others around to the back of the castle. "There's a trapdoor to the cellar here," she said, clearing a few dead berry brambles. "Watch yourself, Rose. These have thorns."

When the door was cleared, Rapunzel yanked it open. Snow went in first. She had to cover her face with her sleeve until she got used to the putrid smell.

"From here we can make our way to the kitchens," Snow whispered, "and from there we can access all the other rooms in the castle."

"What is that awful smell?" Rose asked. Her face was wrinkled in disgust.

"Potion ingredients." Snow shivered. "Let's hold hands so we don't get split up."

"What's all this hanging on the walls?" Rapunzel started to lift her lantern up. "It looks like dead —"

Snow pushed the light down and pulled Rapunzel ahead. She could not bear to see what poor creatures Malodora was torturing for her evil concoctions.

"Good idea. Let's stay focused. We need to get out of here as soon as possible." Rose took Snow's other hand as they made their way up the kitchen stairs.

Nobody spoke as they passed through the greasy kitchen and into the once-grand hallway. Everything was so filthy! The servants must have fled as soon as she had, Snow thought as she ducked under an enormous cobweb. Clearly no one had cleaned the castle in a long time. The smell in the hall was not as strong as it had been in the dungeon, but it was still dank and musty.

Silently the girls took the winding stairs that led to the tower chamber where Malodora kept her mirror.

I hope she hasn't moved it, Snow thought. The last thing she wanted to do was spend extra time in the castle searching in the dark. But they had to find that mirror and get it away from Malodora. Her father's life could depend on it. Slowly she opened the door to the chamber. *Creak.* Snow crossed her fingers. The mirror *had* to be there. Snow almost giggled. Who ever would have believed she would *want* to see that nasty glass again!

Slowly Snow let out her breath as the sliver of moonlight from the tower window confirmed her hope and her fear. The mirror was there, right where it was when she'd lived in the castle.

"Shhh," Rose hushed the girls. A grumbling, growling noise echoed in the stairwell.

"What is it?" Ella whispered.

"The mirror." Rapunzel pointed. "I think it's . . . snoring!"

The giant looking glass was perched on an easel in the center of the room and was clearly asleep.

"It's huge," Ella said.

"And powerful," Rose reminded them. "Let's not wake it."

"How will we carry it?" Ella asked. It was a question Snow had been dreading.

"Carefully," Rapunzel hissed. "Now pick a corner."

Slowly the four girls maneuvered the snoring mirror until it was horizontal.

"Okay, all together now," Rapunzel instructed. "Let's walk in sync and lightly. Waltz rhythm. One-two-three, two-two-three."

Snow felt her feet start to move, and though she was straining under the weight she somehow felt lighter. Halfway down the stairs she started to believe they might actually make it!

"Three-two-three, four-two-three." Rose quietly kept up their count on the dark stairs. But suddenly Snow heard a step out of time. *Did Ella slip?*

No! The harsh scraping sound of hard soles on stone was familiar, but it was not friendly.

"Malodora!" Snow screamed and dropped her corner. Then Ella slipped for real, taking Rose down with her. Rapunzel could not hold the heavy mirror on her own. It crashed to the foot of the staircase. The sound of glass shattering against marble was drowned out by the howl of the mirror itself. Then everything was silent.

Standing in a mess of shattered glass and broken frame, Malodora raised her arms. "Devil's fire!" she screamed. Poor Snow could actually feel the heat of her stepmother's fury and put her arm up to protect her fair skin.

Heat rippled off the queen as she surveyed the destruction of her most powerful tool. She seemed paralyzed with rage.

"Come on!" They hadn't a moment to lose. Rapunzel grabbed Snow. Snow grabbed Ella. Ella grabbed Rose and the girls ran as quickly as they could down the stairs and past the fuming Malodora.

Heat scorched Snow's arms and ankles as she passed her stepmother and kept on running. When they reached the hall Snow glanced back and hesitated. She couldn't leave the castle without taking the mirror, even if it meant picking up the pieces at Malodora's feet. Snow squared her shoulders. But before she took a step, she saw flames shoot from the corridor . . . and then a giant fireball erupted toward them!

The four girls raced through the castle and burst out the front entrance. The cold night air had never been so welcome. Snow ran through the darkness behind Rapunzel, taking in huge lungfuls of cold air until she felt she would burst. She hadn't been this terrified since the night she'd fled the castle and ended up with the dwarves. Finally her feet failed her and she fell to the soft earth. A moment later her labored breathing turned to sobs.

"I failed," Snow cried. "Father is lost to me forever." She let the tears flow. She felt sure that the secret to the curse lay within the looking glass, and any hope she had of lifting the spell had shattered with the evil mirror.

Chapter Fourteen
Last Hope

Snow buried her face in her arms and sobbed into the damp earth. She had never felt so helpless in her life.

"It will be all right," Ella said softly, stroking her hair. "Maybe breaking the mirror will break the spell."

Snow sat up. "Do you think so?" she asked.

Her friends all nodded as they dried her tears and tamped out the embers that still glowed on her gown.

"Breaking the mirror certainly didn't hurt. Malodora sure was angry enough," Rose pointed out.

Rapunzel grinned. "You mean she's not always that charming?"

Snow wiped her eyes with the singed edge of her skirt and tried to smile at the three princesses around her. "Thank you," she said softly. Even if their plan hadn't worked, she was glad to have her friends by her side. "I couldn't have even set foot in that dungeon without you."

"Don't mention it." Rapunzel helped Snow to her feet. "Now let's get you home."

Snow took a last look over her shoulder at the glowing orange sky. Malodora must have set the whole castle aflame! Her old home was truly destroyed now. Not for the first time Snow felt grateful for her cozy cottage and the seven little men who cared for her. They were almost as good as a real father.

Almost. Snow shuffled down the path. She did not want to let on to her friends how disappointed she felt.

"Dear Snow, don't despair." Ella knew what Snow was thinking whether she said anything or not. "We won't stop trying. We'll think of another plan."

"And the spell really might have broken with the mirror," Rose said. She looked up at the sky. The sun's first light was breaking through.

They were almost at the fork in the path when the woods started buzzing. "What in the world?" Ella ducked as a giant glowing bug buzzed past her head. Several more bugs circled the girls, forcing them to stop in their tracks.

Rose's fairies!

"Oh, Rose!" Petunia cried in a blur of orange light. "You scared us half to death." The tiny pixie pulled Rose by the ear. Rose brushed her off, sending her end over end through the air.

"Oh, you don't know scared," Rose said, clearly annoyed.

"Just look at you!" Tulip darted just out of reach, clucking her tongue. "We can't let your father see you like this."

Buttercup tried to wipe a black smudge from Rose's face. "Have you been burned, my dear? Oh, it's just too dreadful!" The poor fairy looked as though she might cry.

"I guess I'd better get home and cleaned up before breakfast," Rose admitted with a sigh. She gave Snow a long hug. "My fingers will be crossed for you," she said in Snow's ear. "And I'll see you in a few hours at school."

Snow nodded and crossed her own fingers as Rose was whisked away, the fairies still fretting colorfully around her.

Ella watched Rose go and looked worriedly toward the horizon. The sky was beginning to lighten. "I suppose I had better get home and get breakfast started. Kastrid has a temper in the morning. Nothing like Malodora's, mind you, but —"

"Go on," Snow said. She didn't want her friends to get into any more trouble for her sake. They had already done so much. "I'll be okay. And thank you."

Giving Snow's hand a last squeeze, Ella left Snow and Rapunzel standing alone on the path.

"I'll escort you the rest of the way," Rapunzel said, slipping her arm through Snow's. "Mother Gothel couldn't care less about when I get home or what state my gown is in. Actually, she might be rather proud of my new look." Rapunzel smoothed soot over her skirt and patted her dirty mass of hair. "And I've *never* cooked breakfast," she joked.

Snow felt relieved. She was starting to really hope her father's memory might have returned. She needed a friend with her when she found out.

The morning doves cooed as Snow walked the last few steps to the cottage and pushed open the door.

"There you are." Mort was stirring a pot of oatmeal over the fire. "Just washing up?" he asked cheerfully. "Oh," he said, turning around and seeing the soot-stained girls. "I think you missed a spot or two."

"Several spots," Rapunzel confirmed. Snow giggled nervously. Her father was not in the room. He was probably still asleep.

"You look terrible," Gruff grumped. Snow shook her head and smiled. Gruff never minced words.

"A cup of tea might help." Meek put two steaming mugs on the table before ducking behind a chair and peeking back at the girls. Wheezer added honey to the mugs between sneezes and Snow and Rapunzel took their seats.

Rapunzel took a sip and chatted with Dim. Nod

snored softly beside her. Snow could not utter a word. It was all she could do not to run upstairs, shake her father awake, and ask, "Do you remember now? Do you remember your own Snow?" She could not even eat. She just sat and stirred her oatmeal and hoped.

At last, just when Snow could bear it no longer, the whole table was interrupted by a loud *WHACK*.

"I'll never get used to that low beam!" Snow's father moaned, covering his face with his hands. Wheezer covered his face, too, but his sneeze sounded a bit like a snicker.

"Oh, Father, are you all right?" Snow rushed to his side.

"Just fine, dear Snow," the man said as he rubbed his tender head. "But I really must insist that you call me Uncle."

"Of course." Snow gulped. She blinked back her tears but could not stifle the sob that escaped her throat as she slumped back on the bench. Her last hope had just been dashed.

Chapter Fifteen
Miraculous Bloom

Rapunzel watched as King White's dark eyebrows knitted together with concern and he gently put a hand on Snow's arm. "Why, whatever is the matter, dear girl?" he asked. He swung a leg over the long bench that ran alongside the table and sat down next to Snow.

With a loud sniffle, Snow lifted her face to look at him, then burst into fresh tears.

Hap pushed Snow's mug of tea closer to her. "Try a sip of tea," he offered.

Snow looked down at the steaming mug but didn't take a sip.

Rapunzel felt terrible. She desperately wanted to help her friend, but could not think of a single way to do so.

"You should eat something," Rapunzel said softly. "We have to leave for school soon."

"School?" Snow said absently, looking up. Her pale

face was blotchy and her eyes ringed in red. "I think I might stay home today," she said haltingly.

Rapunzel frowned. From the very first day of Princess School, Snow had adored attending. She was always babbling about how fascinating it was to learn about becoming a proper princess. Most of the time the idea of becoming a proper princess made Rapunzel roll her eyes. But at the moment she would have loved to hear praise of Princess School come out of Snow's mouth.

Not that she could blame her for not wanting to go. Knowing that her father would never remember her or know who he was, Rapunzel supposed, would make school seem . . . pointless.

"No, dear," Mort said. "You must go to school. Why, your friends and teachers would miss you terribly if you didn't."

"I suppose," Snow said absently. "If you say so."

"Good, good," her father said, patting her hand. He looked over at Hap, who was at the kitchen counter. "Could I have a glass of cider, please?" he asked.

Hap pulled a mug off the shelf and tipped the cider jug over it. Nothing came out.

"Seems we're all out of fresh cider," he said sheepishly.

"Some tea, then?" King White asked politely.

Hap nodded and poured a cup. As he carried it to the table Dim absentmindedly stuck his foot out. Hap tripped and the tea flew. Fortunately Snow's father leaped to his feet, escaping the hot liquid just in time.

Hap hurried to retrieve a kitchen towel to mop up the mess. Rapunzel looked at each of the dwarves. They were suddenly gazing very intently at the floor.

The room was strangely silent. Rapunzel cleared her throat. What everyone needed was something to feel good about — something positive. She drummed her fingers on the table and looked around, thinking. Her mind was blank. Then, out of the corner of her eye, she spotted the singed apple branch still sitting in a glass on the table.

"Look at that!" she said cheerfully. "That burnt stick is actually starting to bloom!"

King White smiled approvingly. "It just needed a little clean water and some minerals from the sea."

Rapunzel peered into the water and saw a few small tendrils of seaweed floating in it.

Snow reached out and touched the apple blossom with her fingertips, but her expression did not change.

Rapunzel leaned in close to Snow. "At least the mirror is broken," she reminded her softly. "Malodora won't be able to watch you anymore."

Snow nodded, tears running down her pale cheeks.

King White patted Snow's arm and leaned forward

to smell the new apple blossom. Closing his eyes, he inhaled deeply. "I love the smell of apple blossoms more than any other flower," he said, sighing contentedly. "I wonder why that is. . . ."

Snow sobbed, and Rapunzel's heart went out to her. If only he loved his daughter as much, or had an inkling of why apple blossoms were so sweet to him!

Rapunzel put a comforting arm around her friend's shoulder as King White opened his eyes. He blinked several times and looked around a bit confusedly.

"I used to have a large apple orchard of my own," he blurted, staring at the single blossom on the table. "But . . . but now this is all that's left of it."

He turned and gazed at Snow. "Dear, dear, sweet daughter," he said, his eyes twinkling. "I cannot bear to see you look so sad."

Snow stared up at her father, her mouth agape. Her face was still reddened and blotchy, but Rapunzel could see that her dark eyes were filled with joy and disbelief. Rapunzel felt relief wash through her as the reality of what was happening hit her.

Malodora's curse had been lifted!

Chapter Sixteen

Happy Reunion

"Father!" Snow cried, embracing him tightly. "You're back!"

Around the table Snow could see the alarmed looks on the dwarves' faces, but even that didn't take away from her happiness. Her father's memory had been restored.

King White hugged his daughter tightly. "We should never be separated. But what strange dreams I've had," he murmured into her black hair. "The sea was so stormy. . . ."

"Oh, Father, it wasn't a dream!" Snow cried, not wanting to think about how awful the whole thing had been. "It was a nightmare come true!"

"Come true . . ." her father repeated. He sat silently for a few more minutes, hugging his only child. Rapunzel remained at the table, beaming and a little bit teary. But the dwarves excused themselves almost immediately. Wheezer and Meek busied themselves with breakfast cleanup. Gruff grumbled to himself while he paced back and forth near the door. Mort and Hap whispered quietly to each other near the fireplace. Dim stared, his eyes wide, at Snow and King White. And Nod couldn't sleep.

Snow wanted to comfort them, to tell them everything would be all right. There was enough room in her heart for each and every one of them. But she also wanted this reunion embrace with her father to last a few moments longer. She smiled over her Father's shoulder at Rapunzel, whose smile was nearly as big as her pile of hair. Snow squeezed her father tighter and he kissed her forehead. Then he sat up straight, scowling.

"That Malodora," he bellowed, pounding his fist on the table. "Keeping me away from my only daughter and destroying my orchards. Who does she think she is?"

"Oh, Father! She is a terrible sorceress!" Snow exclaimed with a shiver. "We tried to steal the magic mirror to break her awful spell and she caught us. When we broke the mirror she was so furious she burned the castle. Your home is in ruins!"

"You tried to steal the mirror?" he asked, shocked. "From that awful castle . . . for me?" King White looked touched and horrified at the same time. "Thank goodness no harm came to you. And do not fret, child. I care nothing for my castle," King White declared. "It is you I cherish, my only daughter. How could she send me away from you? Out to sea forever . . ." he trailed off as his eyes widened. "At sea! I've left my crew out at sea! I must go and rescue them!"

While a few of the dwarves perked up, Snow felt her own face fall. "But Father, I've only just gotten you back!" she said. "I can't possibly say good-bye. I shall never leave your side again!"

King White took Snow's hands in his own. "I know, my sweet Snow. But I can't leave my crew out there adrift. I was once a simple king. But now, for better or for worse, I am a sea captain as well. I must return to sea to find my crew."

Snow nodded, filled with both sadness and pride. Her father was a good, honest man. She knew he was doing what he had to do. And she would do what she had to do as well.

Mort stepped forward. "We have a friend who builds ships," he said. "I'm sure he'd sell you a seaworthy vessel for a fair price."

King White smiled. "Thank you. If you can tell me where his shop is I will go find him. Then I will go to Princess School and explain things to the headmistress.

I should set sail as soon as I can. I would go tomorrow if I could."

"Tomorrow!" Snow exclaimed. Her mind was in a flurry. Her father was finally back and now he was preparing to leave.

There was only one thing to do. Snow would have to go with him.

Chapter Seventeen
Far from the Tree

"Where are they?" Rose murmured, anxiously scanning the lane for a sign of her friends. She'd been waiting on the bridge for what seemed like forever, and there was still no sign of any of them. Tapping her foot impatiently, she felt annoyed with herself for not warding off her fairies after breakfast. She should have rushed straight to Snow's cottage to find out what was happening.

Rose was considering running up the path toward Snow's cottage now when she finally spotted Snow and Rapunzel coming up the lane. Their heads were bent close together and they were walking more slowly than usual. Rapunzel looked a bit silly in one of Snow's gowns, but at least it was clean. And something else was different, too: Snow's father was not with them!

Sprinting off the bridge, Rose rushed up to her friends. "Where is Thornbury?" she asked, a little breathless. "Shall I check the labyrinth?"

Snow was about to reply when Ella hurried up behind them. "What happened?" she asked.

Rapunzel nodded toward the Princess School steps. "We should sit down," she said. "This is a story that needs a little telling."

"Oooh, what a wonderful idea!" Snow agreed as she led the girls toward the polished marble steps. "I love a good story. I just wish every tale could have a happy ending."

Rose felt a tingle run up her spine. It sounded as though the news was good. But Snow's face still looked . . . conflicted. What was going on?

The four girls sat down together on the bottom step. Snow gazed at each of her friends in turn, as if she wasn't sure where to begin.

"Well?" Rose finally asked. She was dying to hear everything! "Tell! I feel like I'm sitting on a whole handful of peas!"

Snow sighed, with a funny little smile on her face, then told them about the return of her father's memory. When she was finished, she slumped back against the second step, looking a little exhausted.

"The apple blossom broke the spell?" Ella said, her green eyes wide. "That's amazing!"

"It's wonderful!" Rose jumped up and threw her arms around Snow. "I'm so happy for you!"

"I'm happy, too." Snow nodded. But a moment later a fresh wave of tears streamed down her face.

"Then why are you crying?" Rose dabbed at Snow's cheeks with her pink hanky.

"You'd better sit back down," Rapunzel said rather solemnly to Rose. "The story's not over yet."

Smoothing her skirts, Rose looked from Snow to Rapunzel to Ella and back. What more could there be to tell?

"Now that Father has his memory back, I've pledged never to let him leave me again," Snow gulped.

"Of course." Ella nodded.

"But father is a man of the sea now, and along with his memories of me, he remembered that his crew is still adrift somewhere. We're leaving to rescue them as soon as possible. I'm going on a sea voyage." Though she was smiling, Snow's eyes were still brimming with tears.

Leave! It was the last thing Rose had expected to hear. She wanted to shout, "You can't leave!" but stopped herself. It was clear Snow was in terrible turmoil and Rose could understand why. Even though her own parents drove her crazy, being away from either of them for a long time would be terribly difficult — it was almost as difficult to imagine as being without her friends.

A lump grew in Rose's stomach. Princess School without sunny Snow was unthinkable. And by the looks on Ella's and Rapunzel's faces, Rose could tell they felt the same way.

"But," Ella began, "we'll all be miser —"

"We'll all be missing you," Rose interrupted, shooting Ella a look. "But the most important thing is that you're happy." Rose knew this decision was hard enough for Snow without her friends making her feel guilty, too.

"A life at sea," Snow mused. "Just think of all the sea animals I'll meet."

Rose strained to be happy for Snow. She forced a smile and lifted her brows at Rapunzel's and Ella's sullen faces, indicating they should do the same.

"I'm sure all the creatures of the sea will adore you as much as we do," Rose said, biting her lip. Then, more quietly, she whispered to Rapunzel and Ella, "If that's possible."

The days passed slowly as Snow and her father prepared for the trip. Rose threw herself into school projects so that she wouldn't have to think about Snow's impending departure. Ella, Snow, and even Rapunzel grew quieter and quieter as the week wore on, each of them spending whatever free time they had together or working on their family trees.

At least our projects will be first-rate, Rose thought as she watched her friends work intently on their embroidery. The family trees were due to be displayed that very day and Rose wasn't sure what would occupy their hands and thoughts once they were turned in. She knew if any of them dared speak about what was really on their minds they would all burst into tears.

"I don't think I can add another stitch!" Rapunzel declared at last. She bit through her embroidery floss, making Rose cringe, and crumpled her family tree in her lap. Just then a trumpet blasted, signaling the start of class.

"Your timing is perfect, Rapunzel," Ella said hurriedly as she added one more row of stitches. "I'm a little late, as usual!"

Folding her finished tree, Rose scooted off the edge of her trunk. Snow stood and the four girls padded down the corridor on their way to Stitchery. As they turned the corner Rose heard a familiar deep voice.

"I'm afraid I will have to retire from my gardening post," the voice said.

The girls whirled around, and saw Lady Bathilde, Madame Garabaldi, and King White deep in conversation.

King White saw the girls as well and gave a small wave and a wink. "Though I have grown quite fond of the beautiful blossoms here, I have urgent maritime matters to attend to."

Madame Garabaldi's face flushed. She looked as stricken as Rose felt.

"I understand," Lady Bathilde said with a small nod.

Rose's hands tightened around her Stitchery basket. If Snow's father was here at school his boat must be ready. He would be setting sail soon and taking Snow with him. Unable to bear hearing those words spoken aloud, she rounded the corner as quickly as possible.

"Our gardens will certainly miss you," Rose heard Lady Bathilde say as she hurried away. They certainly would, Rose agreed. But not nearly as much as she and the other princesses would miss Snow.

In contrast to Rose's mood, the mood in the Stitchery chamber was festive. Madame Taffeta was pacing briskly, her red curls bouncing slightly as she walked. Madame Istoria was also obviously excited about the completion of the joint project. Her brown eyes were bright. As each princess entered she took her tree from her, walked it to the front of the room, and hung it on a dowel. Then, after all of the Bloomers had taken their seats, Madame Taffeta began to call the girls up one by one to present.

Rapunzel was first. "As most of you know, my foster mother is a witch." Rose could hear the pride in

Rapunzel's voice, and in spite of the fact that it was common knowledge she was raised by Mother Gothel, several princesses gasped.

Rapunzel gestured toward her family tree. It was gnarled and lopsided, which suited Rapunzel's sewing style — and her witch family — perfectly. "That's Madame Gothel, of course," she said, pointing to the largest branch in the center. The drab color choices and crooked stitches told much more about the Gothel family than words ever could. "In case you can't actually read it. I wanted the tree to be kind of devilish and witchy, just like Madame Gothel," she finished. The Bloomers applauded politely as Rapunzel took her seat.

After Annabelle and Ariel, Ella was next. She stood a bit shyly at the front of the room and brushed a golden curl from her face before speaking. "I enjoyed finding out about my father's family history," Ella reported, "but by far the most interesting thing I learned in doing this project was that my stepmother was an orphan." Ella pointed to a broken branch on her embroidered magnolia.

Rose could hardly believe her ears. The girls had been so busy with Snow they hadn't had a chance to talk about the other things happening in their lives. Kastrid was an orphan?

"I hadn't known before what a difficult childhood she had," Ella went on. "And it has given me a new understanding."

"Oh, how can she be so awful to you?" Snow spoke out of turn, shocking all of the Bloomers and the two instructors, too. "She knows just what it's like to have no mother!"

Ella nodded. "It's okay, Snow. I understand why she's so awful. Sometimes when you get hurt you want to hurt back. I just hope I can break the tradition."

"You'll break it when you have a daughter of your own," Snow said sweetly. "I'm certain of it!"

"That's exactly right," Rapunzel agreed. "You could never treat anyone badly."

Rose nodded her agreement and Ella smiled at her friends, looking grateful.

"Girls, girls, these are presentations, not forums." Madame Taffeta called the room back to order. "Briar Rose, we haven't heard from you."

Ella took her seat and Rose stood at the front of the room next to her perfectly balanced, perfectly predictable tree. There wasn't much to say about it, but the Bloomers oohed and aahed over her tiny stitches and admired the way she had depicted princes as tiny acorns wearing crowns and princesses as flower buds with dewdrop tiaras.

"Last, Snow White will show us her family tree," Madame Taffeta announced.

Slowly Snow walked to the front of the room. Her project was a bit larger than the others and in truth Rose thought it looked more like a forest than a tree.

"I . . ." Snow's mouth trembled as she began. "I have so many families I had to show them all. Here" — she pointed to a short blueberry bush with lots of branches and even more roots — "are my dwarf papas. This" — she indicated a lovely apple tree with only a few blossoms and its roots in the woods and the water — "is my father's royal family tree. And this" — Snow's chin quivered as she pointed to a rosebush — "is my family of friends."

Rose felt her own chin quake. Snow had included them all in her family!

"But . . ." Snow's voice wavered as she held up a scrap of cloth, a tiny apple. "I just don't know where to put myself!"

Chapter Eighteen

Casting Off

When Snow arrived at the cottage after school, her father was busily preparing for his voyage. Snow had so much she wanted to tell him she wasn't sure where to begin. So she didn't say a word. Instead she began making dinner. She cooked a hearty quiche, three loaves of bread, and a half dozen berry pies.

"A feast!" the dwarves declared as they sat down to supper. But there was little chatter at the table during the meal, and the dwarves hurried off to bed as soon as the dishes were washed. Alone with her father in the great room, Snow wished again she could tell her father what was troubling her. But she could not. Her father, too, seemed to want to say something, but was silent. The silence hung heavily like a branch full of ripe fruit.

"Well, I think I'll be off to bed," King White finally

said. Snow nodded and hugged her father tightly. Then he kissed her on the cheek and went upstairs.

Snow knew she should go up to bed, too. But she also knew she wouldn't be able to sleep.

"Maybe I'll do a little baking," she said to an owl who was perched on the windowsill. "It would be nice to have a few things to eat when we all go down to the harbor in the morning. And perhaps I'll have a little applesauce."

Feeling a little better after a few bites of sweet sauce, Snow got out two dozen eggs, a large chunk of butter, a barrel of apples, and some flour. Humming a slow tune, she began to slice and spice and roll. She made three dozen apple turnovers, four apple cakes, and a giant pan of apple bread pudding. Then she made frittatas and fresh apple cider. By the time she was pulling the last delectable dish out of the oven, the sun was rising over the treetops and several dwarves were coming down the stairs, rubbing the sleep out of their eyes.

"What's this, dear?" Gruff asked, looking over the food that was heaped on the kitchen counter.

"It's for the farewell party, of course," Snow replied. "At the harbor."

"We'll need some wheelbarrows for that," Gruff grumbled as Hap waddled outside to get one. It took half an hour to safely load all the food into a pair of wheelbarrows. Snow packed a couple of picnic blankets into her large satchel. Then, an awkward silence hanging over all of them, she and the dwarves and King White headed to the harbor.

Snow and her father held hands as they walked together along the trail but didn't speak. Gruff, though, did plenty of talking.

"We've got enough pies and pastries to feed a royal army," the grouchy dwarf groused as he pushed one of the wheelbarrows along the bumpy trail.

"We can't set our sailor out to sea on an empty stomach," Hap pointed out as he heaved his own wheelbarrow over a root in the path. "Besides, whatever's left over can go out to sea, too. Along with our hearts," he said softly.

Snow didn't hear him. All she could hear was the voice in her head telling her she needed to say something soon. She was about to open her mouth when she spied her friends waiting down near the water. She dropped her father's hand and ran to them. Surely they would help her say what needed to be said.

"I can't believe you're leaving!" Ella threw her arms around Snow as she approached.

"I can't believe it, either," Snow said, squeezing back. "But that's because I'm not." Snow smiled shyly at her friends.

"You're not?" Rapunzel asked, shocked. "You mean I've been bawling my eyes out for nothing?"

Rapunzel's eyes did look a little red. Snow shook her head. "I just can't leave, not with school and the dwarves, and you . . ."

"Oh, Snow." Rose hugged her, too. "I'm so happy. I just know it's the right decision."

"I do, too," Snow said. "I only hope Father will understand." She chewed her ruby lip nervously.

"You mean you haven't told him?" Rapunzel asked. "Do the dwarves know?"

Snow shook her head and glanced over to the spot on the pier where the dwarves were helping King White load the dinghy he would row out to his ship. Or at least they were trying to help him. Hap kept tipping the water barrels and Gruff was unloading the pies back onto the pier as quickly as Mort was loading them.

"Looks like somebody has been baking," Ella said, noticing all of the food. "Poor Snow, you really have been worried!"

Rose's eyes grew wide and she looked at the piles of pastry and back at her pale friend. "You must have been up all night!" she said.

Snow nodded. "I couldn't sleep," she admitted. "I just don't know how to tell Father I'm not going with him."

"I can't imagine that will be easy," Ella agreed. "But Snow, this time you know he'll come back." The four friends spread the picnic blankets on the grassy bank and set up the banquet. Soon everyone was feasting on Snow's delicious creations.

Snow nibbled on a turnover and watched her father's new ship — a handsome sailboat with a tall wooden mast — bob slightly on the water. She felt terribly proud. But her heart also ached with the knowledge that he would be sailing away without her.

"Your father almost seems anxious to go," Rose said quietly.

Snow had to agree. He was pacing back and forth on the rocks near the sea, mumbling to himself.

"Everyone seems anxious," Snow said, gesturing to the dwarves with her chin. They were clustered together several yards away, looking back and forth between Snow and her father.

Snow leaped to her feet. "It's time to clear the air," she announced. Swallowing hard, Snow walked over to her father.

"Father, there's something I have to tell you," she said, a little louder than she'd intended. The dwarves stopped their nervous chatter and turned toward her. Snow took a deep breath. "I'm afraid I won't be able to go with you," she said.

King White looked a little confused, and Snow felt

a moment of panic. "Out to sea," she added. "I'm sorry. I didn't know how to tell you."

King White stared at his daughter for a long moment. Then he smiled broadly. "Dear Snow!" He swept her up in a hug. "I didn't know how to tell you I think you should stay. As much as I would love to have you with me, you have far too much to keep you here. You must continue your schooling. You have made dear friends. And you will be safe in fourteen loving hands."

Snow let out a giant sigh of relief and threw her arms around her father's shoulders. The dwarves began to dance in circles, singing,

"Hooray, hooray,
Oh, happy day.
Snow will stay!
Snow will stay!"

Ella, Rapunzel, and Rose joined in the dwarves' circle dance as Mort broke away. Blushing like Meek, Mort kicked the ground near King White.

"We're sorry for the way we've treated you, er, sir," he said, holding his hat in his hand. "It's just we thought you might be taking Snow away from us." The other dwarves stopped dancing, too, and came to stand behind Mort.

"We couldn't live without fair Snow," Wheezer wheezed. The others nodded.

"You've taken such fine care of her." King White bowed to the dwarves. "I am forever in your debt."

"Snow will always have a home with us," Gruff said.

"And so will you!" Hap grinned. "We can build you a cabin right next to ours. With a higher roof," he added.

Snow clapped her hands with delight. All eight of her fathers could be together happily.

"But what about the castle?" Gruff asked. "He's already got a home. He doesn't want to stay in some dwarf cabin."

King White grew thoughtful. "The castle was my home once, but home is where your heart is and my heart is with Snow. And my Snow will be with you."

Gruff nearly smiled.

"That castle was cold, anyway," Snow's father added. "Especially with that awful witch in it."

As if on cue, Malodora appeared over the rise, her robes flowing out behind her. She was moving fast and had malice in her eyes. Snow shivered at the sight of her, but her father stood tall and greeted his wife with something like a smile on his face.

"Malodora," he said evenly. "Have you come to see me off?"

Malodora eyed him up and down. "Indeed," she sneered. "Good riddance. I only wish you were taking your daughter with you. But I suppose it's just as well that you leave her here near me."

Snow gasped, and her friends rushed to flank her sides, forming a human shield of protection.

"It will take a fair amount of time to repair the damage you did." Malodora glared at the girls. "But I'll have my mirror back one day. And when I do, I'll keep a sharp eye on Snow — and her little friends, too."

Snow quivered slightly, but Rapunzel raised her chin defiantly. King White put his arm around Snow and the dwarves formed a ring around them all.

King White chuckled. "You can watch all you want, Malodora. Who knows, it may actually do you some good."

Malodora grimaced, repulsed by the loving sight before her. Then, shielding her face, she turned and fled.

"Madame Gothel could teach her a thing or two," Rapunzel fumed.

Ella gave Snow a reassuring hug. "Don't worry," she said softly. "We can handle that nasty witch."

"She's powerless in the face of love. And I will be back to see that she stays away from you." King White patted his daughter's arm.

Suddenly Snow threw herself into her father's arms. Everything was happening so fast. She had been so worried about telling her father she was staying, she forgot that he was about to go!

"Do not fret, dear daughter. Even though you will be staying here, you will be with me, too." He pointed to the stern of his new boat, where he had painted the vessel's name, *Sweet Snow.*

"And if your love was strong enough to bring me home when I was under the control of a terrible witch," he said, his eyes twinkling, "imagine how often it will bring me home when I'm at sea of my own free will."

Wheezer let out a giant sneeze and blew his nose on an already damp hanky. Mort wiped a tear from his cheek. Even Gruff looked touched.

Snow looked around at her father, her friends, and the dwarves — her whole family all together. And in her heart she knew that they would always be with her.

About the Authors

Jane B. Mason grew up in Duluth, Minnesota, where a round stone tower graces the top of the city's hillside. (Fortunately, she was never trapped inside.) She had a strict mother and three older sisters who made her do her share of chores, but never attempted to keep her home from a school dance.

Sarah Hines Stephens grew up in Twain Harte, California, where she caught frogs in the woods but rarely kissed them. She can't talk to birds and she is hardly royalty, but her name does mean "princess," and after dating a toad or two she married a real prince of a guy.

Currently, Sarah and Jane lead charmed lives in Oakland, California. They are great friends and love to write together. Some of their other books include *The Little Mermaid and Other Stories, Heidi, Paul Bunyan and Other Tall Tales, The Legend of Sleepy Hollow, The Nutcracker, The Jungle Book,* and *King Arthur*, all Scholastic Junior Classics, and *The Best Christmas*. Between them Sarah and Jane have two husbands, five kids, three dogs, one cat, and a tomato worm named Bob.

Briar Rose is in a prickly predicament!

When Rose lands the lead in the Princess School play, she is once again the center of attention. But Rose's costar, a fairy named Nettle, can't stand sharing the spotlight. How far will Nettle go to keep Rose off the stage?

www.scholastic.com/princessschool

PS7T

Chestnut Hill

Academics, horsemanship, and rivalries are the course of the day at this exclusive all-girls school in Virginia.

superstars,
d out. But
surprise
mily,
and most of all, herself!

DEAR DUMB DIARY,

In Jamie Kelly's hilarious, candid (and sometimes not-so-nice) diaries, she promises everything in it is true. . .or at least as true as it needs to be.

Available Wherever Books Are Sold

SCHOLASTIC

Learn more at www.scholastic.com/books

FILLGIRL4